A Place of Dreams

A Place of Dreams
The Lough Gur People

ψ

Michael Quinlan

THE O'BRIEN PRESS
DUBLIN

First published 1992 by The O'Brien Press Ltd.,
20 Victoria Road, Dublin 6, Ireland.

Copyright © Michael Quinlan
All rights reserved. No part of this book may be reproduced or utilised in any way or by any means, electronic or mechanical, including photocopying, recording or by any information storage and retrieval system without permission in writing from the publisher. This book may not be sold as a remainder, bargain book or at a reduced price without permission in writing from the publisher.
10 9 8 7 6 5 4 3 2 1
British Library Cataloguing-in-publication Data
A catalogue record for this book is available from the
British Library
ISBN 0-86278-291-0
The O'Brien Press receives assistance from the Arts Council/
An Chomhairle Ealaíon.

Typeset by The O'Brien Press
Cover designed by Michael O'Brien
Cover illustrations Millbrook Studios,
courtesy Shannon Heritage
Cover separations by The City Office, Dublin
Printed by Cox & Wyman, Reading, England

Prologue

There is a lake in County Limerick, a jewel in a fertile plain – Lough Gur, a place of enchantment. Its faces are many and varied. The visible is a display of beauty ever-changing. The hidden lies under lake and hill and is full of mystery and wonder.

The sweep of the lake nearly encircles Knockadoon which was home to the first settlers. The lake waters catch the dark monstrous shadow of Knockfennel on summer evenings. In spring and autumn the sun rises over Drumlaegh (The Grey Ridge) and sets over Ardalugha (The Heights of Lugha).

Lough Gur holds and hides one of the four royal burial grounds of ancient Ireland and is one of the entrances to Tir na n-Óg (The Land of Youth). Ghosts and fairies abound. Watch carefully and the fairies can be seen between sunset and sunrise as they slide on the moonbeams and flit across the waters, or perch on duck or swan to communicate with the rising fish. They live in the green-lighted hollow hills of which Knockfennel is the most populous. It is advisable to avoid Knockfennel late at night because the fairies tend to steal away anyone they might find there. They choose at random from those who stray and most often select one because of his or her goodness and kindness as these qualities are often in short supply in the fairy kingdom and need topping up. It is wise to stay clear of the Red Cellar Cave on Knockfennel, the entrance to fairyland, especially when the moon shines!

Be it the first farmers or the Beaker Folk, builders of great tombs or circles or makers of objects in stone or metal, pagan or Christian, Viking or Norman, landlord or tenant, strong farmer or poor worker, little or great, over five thousand years all have played a part. Memories lie stored within Knockfennel. The red-bearded dwarf, Fer Fi, is the guardian. Listen! It is lucky to hear him laugh and the music he plays on his three-stringed harp can induce joy, sleep or sadness. His 'story' begins when nature had prepared the way and people first came to Lough Gur. A man called Fer was among the first to come ...

* * *

A Place of Dreams is situated in the third millennium B.C., perhaps even a little further back. Dialogue is kept to a minimum, as it is felt it would have been then and violence is not included. When the Beaker Folk come to Loch Gur their culture will introduce bronze, stone-circles, many unusual things and, very likely, violence as well.

During excavation on Knockadoon, which was begun in 1939 by Prof. Seán P. O'Riordáin, the homes of Neolithic people were excavated for the first time. Very little trace now remains of them but the village was there and it is used in the story.

Chapter One

The sky was clear, the sun bright, this was the wind they had been waiting for, and the omens were good. Strong hands pushed the loaded boats out from shore. The sails were raised, the wind caught and the journey begun. On shore, a tribal elder raised the farewell chant. Sen, the wise one, the bearer of knowledge, responded. Back and forth the chant passed, between those left on shore and the adventurers, drifting along the waves and filling the sails, so that the boats strained and groaned with new power.

Though there would be sadness on both sides, those standing on the shore envied those leaving, for they were the chosen ones – the lucky ones. Their going was a tribal decision: overcrowding on the limited good land meant that some must seek out new territories for themselves and future generations. Stories of a rich land, a green land across the seas, were confirmed by the elders who had read the signs clearly in the sacrificial flames. The new land was calling, waiting to share its prosperity with those who were bold enough to seek it out.

Fer was certainly bold enough. The second son of Nar, old and respected leader of the tribe, he was the immediate choice of the elders to lead the expedition. Nar agreed, though he insisted that his third son, Gar, should go as well. Fer had all the qualities of leadership, but Nar could also see where his weaknesses lay, and he knew that Gar's help would be necessary. The time might come when the leadership became Gar's responsibility. Between them they could establish and control the settlement in the new land. Fer then chose equally adventurous companions, each possessing a different and essential skill, each strong and healthy, with a vigorous family. Thus was the complement filled.

Now the voyage was truly underway. The boats sailed in close formation with Fer's vessel slightly ahead, commanding the way, and flanked by three boats on either side, all moving as one. The sun rose higher in the sky and, as the wind increased, so did the boat speed. Fer smiled to feel the breeze in his hair, to hear the creak of timber and leather and the splash of the prow rising and falling as it cut through the waves. He looked to the other boats and saw that all was well. The company of men, women and children were content. So were the animals. Last night, when they had been bound, they had become exhausted in their efforts to free themselves. The loudest protesters had been the cattle, but even they had by now given up the struggle. They lay still, tightly trussed up on the bottom of each boat, where the children would take care of them. And though they would be weak after the voyage of three or four days, they would recover quickly. It would not be any longer than that, Fer hoped. The signs were good.

Day wore into dusk. The sky turned to gold, to red and finally, to the grey of early night. Sen chanted to the setting sun and again the responses swept across the water from boat to boat. Later, when only the helmsman of each boat was awake, the goddess of the night appeared with her followers, the stars in the sky; she reached her high point and moved away as the new day dawned. Fer and the other helmsmen checked their bearings on the stars, as Sen directed, and, satisfied that all was well, they too rested.

Sen was also satisfied. The course was clear – two more sunsets and the new land should come into view.

* * *

It was early afternoon of the second day. Fer would always remember the time. On Fer's orders, Gar had kept to the rear of the fleet, tacking back and forth between the boats with instructions and information, in a craft of superior speed.

What is he doing? Fer wondered, when he noticed Gar's boat had veered wildly off course and fallen far back to port. There must be trouble on board.

Just then, Gar's roar pierced the quiet afternoon air, and the expedition watched the tragedy unfold. Gar was wrestling with a young cow who had broken her tethers. She lashed about in a frenzy of terror. Her sharp hooves punctured the leather hull. Panic broke out on board, and, within seconds, the boat overturned, tossing people, animals and goods into the sea.

Fer gave hurried orders. Frantically, they lowered their sails, turned their boats, and began to row towards the disaster spot. But the cries for help were weaker and less frequent now. And the horrified watchers gazed helplessly as, one by one, Gar's family disappeared beneath the water. Only Gar still struggled. Fer reached him first, and dragged his exhausted body in over the stern of his boat. Now nothing else moved on the surface of the calm sea except the young cow, swimming furiously further and further away, bellowing of her victory in escape and oblivious to the toll of death and sorrow she had inflicted. Only Gar's strength had saved him.

The boats moved close together, as if seeking protection. There was great sorrow. Had not sacrifices been made before they left their homeland? Why had the spirits punished them? How would Gar accept this sorrow? Even Sen had no answer. These things were outside their control. Gar sat hunched in the back of the boat, a warm skin around him. No one could interrupt his mourning. Not even Fer, brother and leader, had a right to interfere.

But the deathsongs must now be intoned, even in this unusual setting, to guide the dead to their new life. What little remained of Gar's property floated on the water and would sustain the dead on their journey. Fer nodded to Sen, and, as they chanted, these last remnants sank to the depths of the sea.

* * *

The voyage continued. But now there was no laughter or banter between the boats. Only the wind, it seemed, remained favourable to them, and that evening they were running before it towards the setting sun. The next morning, Fer came alongside Sen's boat.

'Is it time to change direction?' he shouted across.

'Not until the sun is high above us,' Sen called back, hoping that his judgement was right.

At midday, the boats turned their bows towards the place of the rising sun. Now it was only a matter of time before landfall.

The sun was still high overhead. The sea was a shimmering sheet of silver. And a slack breeze made progress slow, when the watchful eye of Fiar, the hunter, noticed a dark outline on the horizon.

'Land! Land!' he shouted, and all eyes strained in the direction of his pointing finger.

The tension of the past days was over. Fer's woman, Nam, saw the relief on his tanned face and hugged her children happily. 'You have guided us well, good leader,' she said softly. Fer smiled at her proudly. As he looked towards the distant land, he placed a hand on

Gar's shoulder, and for a moment, the emptiness left his eyes.

Slowly, the misty outline took shape. Rugged mountains guarded the land and forests came down to the shore. Fer stood in the bow and gazed in wonder at the bright country. For some time not a word was spoken. Numbed by Gar's loss, Fer's thoughts moved from fear for himself and his companions to expectation. Now that the sea had become their enemy, it seemed of the utmost importance to step on land again. But what did this new place hold for each of them?

At last the boats came to rest on the shore. Sand dunes gave way to coarse grass and behind that lay the thick, seemingly impenetrable, woods. What dangers lurked within? Still silent, each boatload disembarked. The water chilled and then felt warm on their bare sun-hot legs. Three days of hardly moving on board made their muscles cramp and their legs unsteady. Maybe it was that, or the need to touch the new land, that made each sit, or kneel on the shore.

Moments passed, moments of immeasurable time. The water lapped gently, the sounds of the sea and the cries of the sea-birds slipped away, and the bellowing of a stag, and the growl of a bear seemed to welcome them because familiar. And then a new sound mingled with the shore sounds. For the first time, as far as the newcomers knew, the mooing of a cow and the bleating of a sheep were heard in this land, answering the other animals on shore. A surprised silence greeted these new sounds. The native creatures of the forest stopped to listen, and then they came fearlessly from the cover of the trees to look curiously at the newcomers.

Together Fer and Sen stretched their arms upwards, and their voices rose in a high chant. The gods of the sea must be thanked for allowing all but one boat to reach land. All their voices joined together, turning first to the sea and then to their new-found land. They asked the land gods to welcome and protect them, so that they would prosper and increase.

There was much work to be done. The women and children set off to gather armfuls of the plentiful coarse grass from the sand dunes for the animals, while the men, carrying their axes, moved cautiously some short distance inland in search of hunting. They brought back fresh meat and the information that they had landed on the southern shore of a wide estuary. The first stage of exploration had begun.

Alone that evening, Fer paced the sand and thought deeply. The omens were favourable. The time was ripe to continue, for this was not the place of dreams. He would know when they had reached where their destiny lay. They must travel up the inlet, and inland to find the place which had invaded his waking and sleeping hours since the elders had seen his destiny in the stars. Yes, he would know the place when he saw it. It was as real to him as the ground he was standing on now.

After two days of rest, the expedition loaded up the boats again, and let the incoming tide carry them up the estuary.

'We must be careful,' Sen warned. 'When the sea goes out, we must land, or we shall be taken out with it.'

Fer never fully understood why he chose to ignore the first river that flowed into the estuary from the south, or why he chose to follow the second one. Nor did he know why, on the third day, he guided them up the smaller river that branched off to the left. He simply felt that this was right. It was clear in his mind by day and in his dreams by night. They halted that evening when a range of almost treeless hills came into view. Destiny was in sight.

Chapter Two

A rich land, a rich and welcoming land, Fer thought, as he studied the hills that had filled his dreams. Like mighty platforms they towered above a large lake and thick forest, platforms of safety for man and beast. It was a gift from the gods. Tomorrow, they must leave the river and walk across land to the lake. Then they would have arrived. Relieved, Fer fell into a deep and contented sleep.

A cry woke him. The cry of a new-born baby. Fiar's woman, Mas, had given birth to a strong male child, born during the night. His first hours of life were carefully observed, as was the custom. Sen was pleased because the signs were propitious. Fiar looked proud. He had killed a bear last evening, and the smell of its cooking flesh now wafted through the camp. He had been the first to kill, and the first to have a child in this new land. Surely, Fer thought, the gods were smiling on them again, and this new-born boy would one day be a formidable hunter like his father.

Fer looked around the camp. The women were still cooking at the fire, although the men and children were eating the cooked meat, and the dogs sat patiently enough, waiting for their share. Before long, there would be more than enough bones for them. The country was rich, Fer thought, but as far as he had seen, there were no cattle or sheep here. Perhaps there were other people here. His mind wandered to thoughts of home and the people he loved there. His heart sank, he knew he would never return there.

Fer shook himself out of his reverie and sat down beside Sen. Sen was the oldest and the wisest of the expedition. He was highly respected, for he had lived for three decades and seen many changes in the world. For all that, he was in excellent health, and free from the aches and pains that often troubled much younger people. Even though at Sen's age the call to the other world was expected, it was felt that his call was still a long way off.

'Our new land shines in the morning sun. We should be home with the sunset,' Sen remarked.

'Are all the signs good?' asked Fer.

'In the blood of the bear and in the afterbirth of the child and in the signs in the night sky, all augurs well. The gods give us signs of a plentiful welcome,' answered Sen.

Gar sat silently beside Sen. Fer turned to him and spoke quietly: 'Now is the time to take stock of what the future holds. Begin afresh, Gar. Forget your sorrow and accept the will of the gods. You have survived their terrible test. Now you must make another family to replace the one you have lost. As leader of this tribe, I will help you as far as our laws permit. As your brother, I can give you grain and cattle, so you can begin again. But these you must return when you have acquired your own. Par and your children, I cannot replace, but with new possessions, you will find another woman. You know all our women have men, but in a few years Sen's daughter will be grown. Be patient. We may well find other tribes in this land. Let sorrow be gone from your heart, Gar.'

According to tribal law, Gar must accept Fer's offer of help. To refuse would be a weakness and a failure to cope with what the gods had willed. Gar would be disgraced and lose his tribal rank. Heavy of heart, Gar nodded.

'Fer, I accept your offer and will return my obligation to you as soon as I can. When the time is right, I will take another woman, though my heart is sore for Par and my children.'

* * *

Fer was pleased by many things as he surveyed the line of travellers. The animals had recovered fully from the voyage. Freed from their fetters and let loose on the rich water meadows, they frolicked and leaped, noisily announcing their joy. It was the task of the young boys and girls to drive them 'home'.

From the waters of the river to the waters of the lake was but as short distance, but being heavily wooded, it was difficult terrain. Oak and elm stretched towards the sky and the undergrowth was thick with hazel and briar. A twisting track had been hacked through the undergrowth. Some of the stronger saplings were prepared as rollers on which to transport two of the boats. They would be of use to the lake colony, to ferry people and goods to the lush island in the middle of the lake that awaited them.

All was ready. Fer intoned the prayer, and Sen raised the incantations which would ensure good fortune. The ceremonial bones clacked their signal through the air — the signal to break camp. Raising their bundles, the party began the final short trek.

There was no fear. The hunters had already explored the countryside, and found no immediate dangers. The first touches of autumn tinted the leaves. A few had fallen to the ground into a pattern of welcome. Mottled sunbeams pierced the leaves, while in the branches the birds sang contentedly, pausing as the strange entourage passed by.

Chapter Three

'On this island hill, wrapped within the arms of the lake, we will live and prosper,' Fer said.

There it stood, two hundred paces across the water, a grass-covered hill, calling to them to come and live.

'The soil awaits our crops and the pasture our cattle.' Fer was entranced. He had seen the island many times before, but the reality surpassed his dream.

Joy and laughter replaced the silence. It was a happy moment. Sen took stock of the landmarks. To the north rose the highest hill, a shield from the cold wind, to the east and west stood lower hills, while great forests stretched to the south as far as the mountains in the distance. In the middle of all, surrounded by the lake, was the island hill, its two high points flanking a valley.

'When we celebrate, it will be on that summit yonder,' remarked Sen, pointing to the highest peak.

Fiar was responsible for transporting the animals across to the island. He drove them around to the eastern side of the lakeshore, where the island was closest to the mainland and the water was shallow. Here, the cattle could be swum across. The sheep and goats would be loaded back onto the boats and ferried to the other side. From afternoon until evening, the boats ferried people, goods and animals, to the island. There, rough shelters were erected, home until houses could be built. The settlers slept deeply that night.

* * *

'We will build our homes here, where we came ashore,' Fer said to the gathered people on the first morning. 'We will build close together, our people will work together and our animals graze together. Our children will grow strong together. The land will bless us and produce in plenty. We will prosper and our gods will be pleased and will help us.'

Apart from Gar, the men all had a woman and children. Thirty-one people had reached this new homeland and one child had been born since their arrival. Fer knew that he had chosen his party well. They had a good mixture of age and skills and, better still, the men had shared many adventures together, forging a strong bond between them. Each family group had been chosen for its skill in a different craft, crafts which would be essential in setting up a new community. This group would succeed and Fer knew it. Sar, the builder, came forward.

'First, Fer shall choose his site. Then each family will choose its own site,' he said. 'Together, we will build strong and comfortable homes. You will reward me and my family for our knowledge by supplying us with food until the sun reaches its low point and the nights their longest span. Thereafter I will join the hunters.'

It was settled. Each family agreed on a section of level land without bickering of any sort, as if it knew its designated place. Fer's house would be the focal point of the village. Rectangular in shape, it would also be considerably larger than the others. As each family marked off its ground, it seemed suddenly that the voyage was ended, that the anchor had finally been dropped.

* * *

During the weeks that followed, Sar's high-pitched voice bullied, ordered and encouraged the builders.

Smallest of the men, he was probably the strongest of them all, with a squat and powerfully built body. He was extremely untidy, with hair and beard always untrimmed. His face held piercing brown eyes, a nose bent and flattened from twice being broken, and his front teeth were missing. From his neck, suspended on a cord, hung a notched measuring rod, a sign of his trade. He was a man of short temper. Everyone avoided the barb of his tongue, so there were no idlers.

They realised that they were working for themselves as well as for each other. Their houses would grow simultaneously. First, sound foundations were laid by gathering fairly large stones from the land and lakeshore and placing them in the trench which marked the outline of each house. Soon, door openings were visible. Most of the doorways faced south, toward the lake, catching the sunshine by day, and warming the inside of the house. Only the house of Uish, the most skilled tool-maker of their homeland, favoured the morning sun because, as he said, it showed him more clearly the correct line on which to break the stone to find the best quality, while Cre, the one skilled in pot-making, needed the rays of evening sun to dry his day's work.

When the foundations had been laid, posts were secured on either side of the house and bound firmly. Set well into the ground, they extended to roof level and were tied with thongs prepared by the women. Sar had found an ideal grove of saplings on the eastern slope of the hill and had dispatched his workers there. Good axes quickly cut through the saplings and they were brought back to the site to Sar and his family. Tested and pointed they were driven into the ground and tyings were make at three points. The wall height was less than the height of a man as the high-pitched roof allowed plenty of headroom.

Each evening the woodcutters brought their damaged and blunted axes to Uish. He was the earliest to rise, and from first light he was at work, carefully flaking the damaged flint and bringing up a perfect edge. When an axe could no longer be repaired, he converted it into a scraper or knife. There was no room for waste in this community. Often an axe simply needed re-hafting. Luckily, Uish had brought a good supply of well-seasoned timber handles to the new land and could expertly re-haft any axe to the satisfaction of its user. He was also very busy making axes. Although they had carried many axes and other tools with them from over the sea, Uish had made sure to bring the raw material with him, even though it had been difficult and cumbersome to transport. But even so, soon he would have to find a new source.

Each afternoon the women prepared the evening meal for the hungry workers. The hunters had had little difficulty in stocking up enough meat to feed the tribe during building because of the plentiful supply of unsuspecting game. The meat was roasted on spits over the fires and crushed grain was made into flat cakes. Until the houses were built, the tribe would eat together, and, at the end of a good day's work, the meal was a happy affair. Sar, who was satisfied with progress, used the occasion to praise and encourage the youngsters about their day's work. After the meal, the children played their own games by the lakeshore, the men sat around one fire and the women around another and each group discussed its own affairs. Often, when the women and children had gone to the shelters for sleep, the men looked to the stars.

Huddled in warm animal skins, they listened to Sen retell the ancient story of the night and day. The words were old. As they listened they watched the stars travel across the sky, and it was late when Sen finished: ' ... and the god of the sun warms our days. He rests over the edge of the world and the moon's followers stand guard over the night, circling on high, and brightening the darkness, to await the return of the sun. The longer he rests the colder the weather, but the stars shine to tell us that day will always come. It has always been so.'

They gazed at the moon, goddess to the sun, and ruler of the night. Sometimes she was shy and just peeped her presence, at other times she displayed the full-blown beauty that often caused strange behaviour in man. God and goddess, father and mother, protector and protectress, together they dominated the heavens. The men watched, wondered and accepted Sen's explanations, while the women asked for blessing and fertility from the queen as she crossed the sky to meet the sun.

Chapter Four

Custom demanded that on this day the great fire must be lit to salute the waning sun, and acknowledge the bountiful harvest made possible by his power. As yet they hadn't grown any food in their new home, but wild apples, blackberries and hazelnuts were heavy on the shrubs and trees, and they had carried stores of grain from their homeland and the god of the sun had ripened them all.

'We will celebrate as we did at home,' Sen said to Fer, as they sat by the fireside together one evening, discussing the affairs of the day.

'You are now sure of the day?' Fer asked, knowing full well that Sen did not err.

'Five days from today is the day of celebration. Our people at home will be celebrating at the same time. It will bring them close to us and us to them.'

Sen studied the stars' movements, the moon's passages and the sun's position each year to find the exact time that the earth passed into its cold and dark season. From experience, he could quickly establish the day, but in this new land to be fully sure he continued to study the signs until the celebration was just five days off.

'Have you chosen a place?' Fer asked him.

'When we first stood on the lakeshore yonder, I chose the high point of this hill for fire celebration. It will be seen for miles around. If fires appear on other hills, it will mean there are other people here. It is important we make contact with them.'

Both thought of Gar.

'You will decide when to announce the feast, but allow time for the hunters and the women to prepare.'

This was to be their first rest since coming to this

favoured land and Fer knew well that his people deserved the three days of rest and celebration.

Two nights before the feast, Fer called the tribe together. There was great excitement – the people knew that the time of the fire celebration was near.

'My people,' he began, 'as our houses grow, so our roots grow into this new land. Now we are here to stay and generation will follow generation. As a people we will grow strong. The good land gives many signals of welcome.'

Fer paused to stare out over the lake, over the beached boats on to the wooded shore and vast unexplored land beyond. Animal and bird sounds came from land and water, and Fer was happy that all was well.

'Already I can see that thoughts of the old land are fading in the good life here. New people will come and join us and we will welcome them in peace. Untouched land in plenty awaits across the water there, whenever it is needed. The good soil will yield rich harvests.

'But that is in the future. Let us think of the present. It is time to light the great fire to salute the sun's decline. Let him see our great blaze and hear our voices as we call to him. Let us gather fruits and offer them to him. Let us stop work and enjoy well-earned rest. The sound of the bones in the morning will signal the beginning of the celebration and preparations will then begin.'

He paused and watched the delighted expressions on the work-weary faces. 'Tomorrow we prepare and then we will rest and enjoy.'

The cheering startled the lake birds as they settled down for the night. The herons stirred in their roosts on the small island, ducks quacked and moved among the reeds and one pair rose with a clatter of wings, the swans turned their graceful necks to look, neither startled nor afraid. Everyone spoke at once, making plans, remembering other feasts, laughing and talking. Each family wandered back to its own shelter to settle down for the night, but the talking and planning continued until the stars and the moon had passed unnoticed across the sky. Unnoticed by all, that is, except Sen, who was still charting their progress, and Gar, who watched and hoped that by the next celebration of fire, he would no longer be alone. He felt sure that there were others in this land. For many years, people had sailed the sea and not returned. Some must have come here. Perhaps they would see the great fire and make contact. Other people are here, he told himself again and again, until he was convinced.

He looked towards the moon and in his heart he made promises. Promises as to how he would repay the goddess of the night for her help. She was the goddess of all hunters, and would require blood sacrifices. 'I will kill a mighty bear and offer his flesh to you, great Goddess, and on its skins the woman that you send me will conceive brave hunters.' Confident, Gar slept easily that night.

The bustle of morning was somewhat different. The bones announced a break from normal routine. Except for Uish, who was in great demand as the men came to him for axe-sharpening and repairs, before going to the grove in the valley to cut timber for the fire. For many hours the sound of tree-felling echoed around the hills and, as the lengths of timber became ready, the youngsters stood by to haul them up the steep eastern hill to the summit.

Meanwhile, the women and girls gathered the remaining fruits from the trees and bushes. The best of these would be offered in the fire on the following day, in a magnificent pot which Cre was moulding carefully.

Since early morning, Fiar, with Gar, Sar and three

youths, had been out searching for a stag of noble proportions, a worthy offering. For many days, Fiar had watched the movements of a fine stag who came to the lake to drink. Each evening, at much the same time, the stag passed through a narrow gully on his way to the shore. Fiar planned to block the further end of the gully with woven branches, supported on a central post driven into the middle of the path. At the near end, he would set off some loose rocks to tumble down and block off the entrance. As long as the men could prevent the stag's escape up the steep sides of the gully, they could kill the trapped animal with stones and axes.

Preparations were completed and Fiar waited anxiously. If the plan failed, the consequences were dire. The feast demanded fresh meat as an offering and, since Fiar was the chief hunter, if he didn't succeed, Fer could order one of his animals to be killed. Failure would also undermine his rank as hunter in the tribe. They waited nervously. Each man had his weapons ready and his dog by his side. They waited well downwind, in cover, but with a clear view of the gully entrance.

It was late afternoon when the stag approached, alone, as was his wont. He paused at the entrance to the gully and surveyed the terrain, nostrils twitching, head held high. His keen sense of smell was particularly sensitive to bear and wolf scents. As yet he could hardly recognise the scent of humans, but any unexplained smell would be classified as enemy. A bend in the gully prevented the blockage at the end being seen, and Fiar and his men had been particularly careful not to disturb anything at the entrance. The lever under the rock, which would cause the rock-fall and close the entrance, was well hidden.

The stag moved forward slowly, still sniffing but quite unafraid. And then he sped nimbly through the ravine towards the lake. When he rounded the bend, he saw his way blocked. All four feet stopped at once, but his body-weight and the incline carried him forward, slipping on the gravelly slope. He struggled to remain on his feet, made a gallant effort to spring clear of the obstruction, but landed on top of the barricade, striking the centre post with colossal force before falling to the ground, stunned. Amid the pain and fear, he heard sounds that he had never heard before – human voices.

At the very moment the stag had rounded the bend, Fiar had shouted the command. Sar pulled the lever, and the rock and smaller stones crashed down to close off the entrance. He ran to man the slope of the gully as Fiar and Gar dashed into it with their dogs. The stag had risen to his feet, shaking and afraid. His instinct directed him towards the entrance, but shouting men and barking dogs blocked his way. A stone thrown from above struck him on the shoulder as he tried to escape up the side of the gully. Another man stood in his way. Dazed and hurt, he turned to face his enemies. Gar threw his axe, and it struck deep into the stag's forehead. Gar shouted in joy as the stag staggered and fell to his knees. Fiar delivered a second blow, which shattered his skull. The struggle was ended.

The great animal toppled over and lay still. Blood flowed from his forehead and nostrils. The hunters gathered around, somewhat in awe, to pay tribute to the brave beast. Each dipped a hand in the blood and rubbed it on his own forehead and face. Then they dipped again and rubbed the blood onto each other's hands, bonding their friendship with the kill.

'Beast,' Fiar said, 'we salute your bravery with your blood.'

'Bravery with blood,' the others replied.

'Let us imbibe his spirit,' said Gar, the privileged one,

credited with the kill. Later his skill and bravery would be extolled around the campfire.

Fiar drew a sharp flint flake from his pouch and slit the jugular vein. The carcass gave a final twitch and lay still. Hot blood gushed forth and each man cupped his hands, filled them with blood and drank. Blood stained their beards and garments as they wiped their hands on their hair. Now they were hunters and could salute the slain stag and draw his strength and courage to themselves. Each then gave a bellow, and the dogs howled in reply. Those working in the grove and the village heard their victory cries. They stopped work and cheered, raising their hands to the sun.

The solemn moment passed. Blood trickled into puddles around the still carcass, and the dogs licked at it greedily. Fiar bound the stag's legs together, and slid a strong sapling through them, so that the animal could be carried home.

Chapter Five

A great fire beckoned the tribe to the hilltop. Fer and Sen walked at the front of the procession, beating a pace with the bones. Down to the shore they went, then up to the valley and east in zig-zag fashion up the steep slope to arrive at the fire. The women carried the partly cooked stag and placed it over the fire where the flames were damped down. The flesh was covered with scraws cut from boggy soil by the lakeshore and soaked in animal fats, stored from previous cookings. Soon the succulent meat would be distributed among the tribe, and the praise of the hunters, especially Gar, would be sung.

It was a perfectly still evening, and the smoke drifted straight up into the sky. The dancing flames and rising sparks hypnotised the tribe and they stood entranced, gazing into the fire. Gar imagined that he could see the faces of Par and his children in the flames. Others saw friends from their homeland. They whispered imagined conversations with them. Often the faces lingered and the fire-gazers shed gentle tears. Were these people living or dead? The images often brought anguish, but all knew that the contact was broken forever. Such had the gods destined.

Later the women sectioned and served the perfectly cooked deer and the whole tribe sat and gorged on the succulent meat. Tribal hierarchy was maintained: Fer and Sen were served first, but Gar, the provider, received the biggest portion and the cooked heart. Never had the tribe felt closer than at this moment – a unity which almost removed individuality and ensured a continued pooling of talents for the common good. Even the dogs were rewarded with bones cleaned of flesh and tossed over shoulders.

By the great fire, stood Cre's enormous pot, loaded with the choicest products of the land – berries and nuts, apples, plums, sloes, haws and rosehips, acorns, chestnuts and hazelnuts, with withering leaf and branch for decoration. And to combine plant and animal in the offering, the head of the stag was placed on top of the overflowing pot. It was ready to be consumed by the fire and taken up to the heavens.

Meanwhile Fer and the men opened a way into the heart of the fire by pushing the burning logs aside. The task was difficult because of the great heat, but finally it was done. The pot, crowned with head and antlers, was manoeuvred slowly through the passage of fire until it stood at the very centre. Then the fire was closed up again. No fresh wood had been added for some time, so the fire was a huge smouldering mass with little flame. Soon the pot cracked in the intense heat, the leaves and branches took flame and the sizzle of burning fruit and the popping of nuts was heard. The hair on the deer's head singed and sent a new mix of smells rising into the smoke and on up to the sleeping sun. A soft chant of 'Ya, Ya, Ya' continued until all was consumed in the flames. Plenty of meat still remained and now they could eat the produce of the earth too. Bread, nuts and fruit were shared and washed down with the precious wine, brought in skins from across the sea.

Fer and Sen stood a little apart. Moments earlier Sen had seen a falling star and was well pleased. Others had seen it too and spread the word among those who hadn't. Happiness prevailed.

'Now that we have made the offering, this land becomes more our own,' Fer remarked.

'The signs speak well, Fer, and the shooting star is the best sign of acceptance of our offering,' Sen replied.

'And now the moon crowns the night.'

'We have chosen well.'

They noticed Gar standing alone, studying the landscape. Both knew what was on his mind.

'Were it not for Gar's loneliness, all would be well. He needs a companion. He's hoping that fire will appear on another hill. I'm surprised too, that we haven't seen light before now,' Sen added.

'I am sure,' said Fer, 'that there are other people here. Before long, I feel that we will see flames on some hill near or far. But we must be cautious. This land is now ours. Others might be welcome, but it would depend on what they might offer in skills and friendship.'

Gar joined them. 'Is it not strange that no fires appear on the distant hills?' he asked.

'We have just noticed the same thing,' Sen answered, 'but consider, Gar, that the others may be watching our fire and wondering who we are, since light has not shone from this hill before. Let us wait, perhaps fires will appear.'

But first it was time to dance. The music started up. The rhythm was quick and the horns gave short blasts, the bones beat faster and faster. Little by little the people began to move, swaying gently and then circling around the great fire. Mas clutched her young son to her breast and began to dance. A low chant rose in time to the beat, at first barely audible, then growing louder and louder. The chant was old and used words of thanks as well as sounds which not even Sen understood, so old were they. Louder and faster the bones clacked, louder and faster rose the chanting, faster they circled the fire. The younger children grew tired and sat down exhausted on the grass. The mothers passed the infants to them, almost without altering rhythm or movement. Still the pace quickened. Faces and bared limbs glistened with sweat in the firelight. Suddenly Sen raised his staff, and the dancers stopped breathlessly, frozen in position. This was the moment of contact with the sun, the offering of themselves at one with the flames, begging the sinking god to fall no lower in the sky. Sen's staff pointed to the sun, and all stood facing it with hands extended and palms upturned as if to hold and support the sinking sun.

A short blast on the horn shattered the solemn silence. Immediately the young bone-beaters struck a beat. Slowly, as if waking from a dream, movement began again. Round and round, lighter and happier, bodies swayed and leaped, turning and twisting, now shouting and screaming as the music quickened. Faster and faster, faster than ever before, until their actions became frenzied gyrations. Unconscious of themselves or their surroundings, they fell and rolled on the ground. They fell on stones and bled, they leapt the flames and walked on burning sticks. Garments caught fire and were quenched with bare hands without pain. Their eyes glazed and the tempo reached a crescendo, and each body forced itself to its limits. When the music stopped again, oblivious to all else, male and female reached for each other and collapsed onto the ground, locked in embrace.

* * *

Gar was thoughtful. Today had been special. His spirit had stirred again for the first time since his loss at sea. The blood and heart of the stag had fired him. He wanted life again and someone to share it with. His body ached for a companion. He had been excluded from the fire dance, and had watched sadly as the couples had mated. He was envious now of the families as they bedded down for the night around the blazing fire. He volunteered to stay awake to tend the fire. Soon the others slept.

Gar's heart missed a beat. Quietly, he went to Fer and shook him awake. Fires had appeared on two distant hills, very far away, but definitely fires. Minutes later, a not-too-distant hill was crowned in flame. Together Fer and Gar watched the hill fires and Gar's loneliness diminished.

Chapter Six

Neither Fer nor Gar mentioned the late night fires the next day. No one else had seen them and for reasons they could not explain, they felt they should keep them secret, for the moment at least.

Instead, Gar crossed the lake to the mainland to explore in the direction of last night's closest fire, but he soon returned. The thick forest was forbidding for a man alone. Perhaps the fire-people of the not-so-distant hill might also be searching to make contact with the newcomers. Gar would have to wait.

Sar and Uish decided to spend this rest day exploring the hill together with their women and children. They had always been close friends and their women were sisters. Both women were tall, almost as tall as their men, which was unusual. Their long hair fell to their waists, and each carried a baby at her breast, while her other children ran along behind. They wore tunics which extended to the ankle and a shoulder cloak of animal hide. The tunics were brown and woven in good style. At home both women had learnt the skill of weaving from their parents, and, in this new land, cloth-making occupied much of their time. As today was a special occasion, each wore a necklace of seashells and bracelets. Sar's woman, Yan, wore one of blue stone, for which Sar had once traded two goats. Ish, Uish's woman, wore a red polished stone, a gift from Uish.

Together they walked toward the western point of the hill. There was a slight chill in the air, but the sun shone brilliantly as if in gratitude for the offerings of the night before. The grass was burnt by the frost and most of the leaves had fallen from the trees. But the lake was resplendent, sparkling blue with a gentle ripple. It was home to many breeds of birds, which bobbed on the waters in their hundreds and thousands, their calls filling the air. From this height, they could see the place from which they had sailed across from the mainland to the island in line with the setting sun. They sat on the stones and gazed at the beauty that surrounded them.

The point was thickly wooded and on the hill there was a fair number of trees, but they were mostly quite small and would be used for burning during the winter. Uish and Sar walked ahead and led the way across a ridge, climbing higher and admiring each unfolding scene. They stood on top looking down into the valley. The drop was sheer and, on a crag close to the top, was the eyrie of a pair of golden eagles. When they heard the voices above them, the eagles rose majestically in the air, casting alarming shadows with their huge outstretched wings. The women hugged their babies tighter and the young children clung to their legs in fear. The shrill call was a warning and the men knew that these birds could well be dangerous enemies. It was time to move down into the valley.

The sun shone on the valley and it was warm and sheltered from the breeze. Possibly formed when an ancient cave system collapsed, the layers and folds of the rock formation were visible in places towards the top. Uish's pulse quickened when he noticed a glint as the sun struck the rockface. Quickly, he climbed up the slope and went on his knees to examine the uncovered rockface. He let out a shout of pure joy. The rock contained layers of stone and in alternate layers were black nodules. Chert, not as good as flint, but an adequate material nonetheless. This, he knew, could be fashioned to make tools. He knew that he could work with it and he was overjoyed.

'Look! Look!' he shouted to the others. 'Now I can

make all the things we need. No more shortage of blades, scrapers or axes. I can even make fishing-spears.'

'It is good, Uish,' Ish beamed.

Sar was delighted too. 'I want an axe of the blackest stuff and for Yan a bracelet of black stone.'

'All in good time,' Uish agreed happily.

But today was not a day for work and they walked back to the eastern hilltop where the remains of last night's fire still smoldered. Much of the ashes had been scattered, leaving only a heap in the centre on which the skull of the deer lay. Much of the carcass also remained, and, when darkness fell, the wild creatures of the hill would feast on it. The adults sat and talked while the children played. Remembering the activities of the previous night, they played as they had seen their elders play, dancing round and round. One of them picked up two bones and struck a rhythm. Later, happy and exhausted, they joined their parents and all feasted on bread and fruit.

Across the water on the mainland, great wooded plains stretched from the lake to the mountains, some very far away. Furthest away two perfectly symmetrical cone-shaped peaks were just visible.

'Woman mountain,' Uish laughed, pointing. Sar smiled.

Both women were feeding their babies. Well-nourished infants who sucked aggressively so that dribbles of milk and spittle flecked their mothers' exposed breasts.

'Mother Earth will yield to us as we yield to our children,' Yan said quietly to Ish, not wanting the men to hear.

'And we'll all grow strong on her bounty,' Ish replied, as she shifted the hungry infant to her other breast, a move that raised a howl of annoyance from him.

As they admired their new and vast land, Yan called their attention. 'Can you see it?' she asked, as she pointed to a streak of silver on the north-western horizon.

'Surely it is the mouth of the great river where we entered from the sea.'

She was right. They gazed in stunned silence. It was an entry point, but it could also be an exit point and its location was important to know. Now it also seemed a link with home and brought painful memories of loved ones and of days past. A lone cloud crossed the sun and startled them from their reverie.

'Soon more people will come and find their way here to us. They will come by the great river,' Sar said.

'We have travelled far from that river mouth, but all is well and this land is good to us,' replied Uish.'Yes, Sar, others will come and our children will mingle with theirs. Together they will fill this land, clear the forest for pasture and raise great herds and they will prosper.'

It was time to return to camp and they descended slowly by the northern face to reach the shore. As the sun sank lower in the sky, the water turned to gold and its beauty filled them with contentment. Slowly and dreamily they walked along, the children dawdling behind. To the left a pathway went straight up the hillside to a cave-mouth. Isht and Saru, two of the bigger children, noticed it and nodding silently to each other, slipped away to explore.

Uish always said that Isht should have been born a boy. She spent all her time with them and especially with Saru. They would form a family one day, but they still had some growing to do first. She was the only girl who ever went out with the hunters. She had been there when Gar killed the stag for the feast.

'Come on, Saru,' she pleaded.

'We don't know what's in there,' he said, hesitating. 'Maybe the gods of the other world will draw us and keep us there forever.'

Isht laughed and taking his hand, pulled him forward, her playful eyes shining in her little white face.

'The god of the cave might be glad to see us,' she joked, as they stood at the mouth and peered into the darkness. But the hair rose on their dogs' backs and they began to growl. An answering growl came from within, echoing and re-echoing. The children ran in fear, as a huge brown bear ambled sleepily to the cave mouth.

'You can kill him for me,' Isht whispered to an incredulous Saru when they were a safe distance away.

For all the wonder of the day, it had also uncovered two formidable enemies.

Chapter 7

Sar was aware of other building techniques, but he chose the style for which the materials were most convenient. He ordered turf to be cut in the wetter areas of the shore, areas which would be submerged in winter. The sods were cut wide and deep and packed tightly together to make walls stout enough to keep out the strongest gale. Reed was plentiful too and easily gathered with a sharp sickle. Once the walls were built, ashes from the fire of celebration had been placed on top and above the doorway to protect the house from burning and to keep illness without. This evening the last reeds were being placed, and tonight they would all sleep in their new houses.

Sar allowed himself a moment of pride and walked up the hill to look down on the completed village. It fitted well into the hillside and each house looked snug under its reed cap. The roofs extended out over the walls and Sar thought that from a distance they looked like a cluster of pointed mushrooms. Of the seven houses, Fer's was the largest and would serve as a meeting place during the cold winter months. As Sar climbed higher, they seemed to snuggle even closer into the hillside. The evening was still and soon he saw smoke seeping through the thatches, not rising as smoke rises from a fire in the open, but coming through all over the roof as if it was about to take flame. He had often thought of leaving an opening for the smoke, but then the rain and wind would come in. This way the smoke gathered in the roof area, some went out through the doors, but most seeped through, and within, if one kept low, it didn't sting the eyes. Because she was tall though, Yan had difficulty keeping below the smoke and she often complained. There must be a better way.

Some houses had been ready for a while, but they hadn't been used, as it was understood that all would be occupied at the same time. Many of the men were now able to stand back and admire their contribution with pride. After so many weeks of communal work, perhaps they were regretting the return to family activity. But this would not begin until spring.

Yan's house was beautiful, she thought, and she would make it more beautiful. Now the inside was quite bare. Sar had paved the hearth with water-worn stones which he had found in the lake. Had he not known better he would have been sure that they were part of an ancient pavement, but where could it have led to and who could have built it? Anyway, it now made a fine hearth.

Rough bed forms stood by the walls and the thick hides which had kept them warm while sleeping out of doors were more than adequate indoors. The hides that had formed the tents now lined the inner walls and so made the home more comfortable. Rough stools completed the furnishings. Large clay pots stored all the necessities of daily life. One container would remain untouched until the following spring – the one in which the seed for next year's crop was stored. But the fire was the real heart of the house, giving light and heat, welcoming and cheering. In deep winter the animals were often brought in and provided another source of heat. But fire could also be a terrible enemy, especially if it made contact with the roof. Life was often lost, life and possessions, and much sorrow was caused.

Yan's most precious possession was the frame of timber which stood beside their bed. Sar had made this simple loom for her as a marriage gift. The workmanship was excellent, especially the many pins on which the threads wound, which he had fashioned from bone. Each could be removed when the cloth was made.

Fiar had crossed the hill to watch the movement of animals down to the water's edge at evening time. He lay hidden in the trees halfway up the hill, where he had a good view of much of the shoreline. The deer were very plentiful. This was the time of the year when the stags shed their antlers, and so there was little to differentiate between stag and hind until the male called to the others of the herd and his thunderous bellow filled the air. Fiar picked up a fine set of antlers, cast where a stag had rubbed them on a tree. It was a useful material. He hoped to find many others during hunting trips.

As the shadows lengthened, flocks of birds circled above and then came to rest on the water, skimming the surface with their out-turned webbed feet before plopping to a stop. Now they were mostly duck from further north, but he thought that the bigger birds would come too, as they did in their homeland. When the geese came he would arrange a hunt on a night when the moon did not shine. He turned homewards. He looked forward to being in his new home tonight. As chief hunter, he had many hides on his walls and, like pictures, each one told a story. Now he could lie on his bed and re-live the many chases. The hides proved that each had ended in success, but the cost had often been heavy and some also told of lost friends who did not live to celebrate the kill. One such was the big bear skin which held pride of place in his home, because it was a memory and a warning – a memory of his dead father who had been killed in that hunt and a warning of the dangers of the bear. He thought then of the bear or bears in the Cave of the Echoes. He would have to kill them. They could not share the same hill.

Sar turned around and saw Fiar striding up the hill

towards him. He waited. Without any shortness of breath, Fiar stopped beside him. A mighty hunter indeed, thought Sar, as he greeted Fiar.

'If you are admiring your work, Sar, you have every reason. Everything fits perfectly in place and nobody need now fear the winter. There is no better shelter in the world!' said Fiar.

Sar was often praised for his skills but, looking at Fiar, he felt a twinge of regret that he wasn't the hunter. 'Yes, Fiar, of course I am happy with the work done, and the effort we all made, but my work is done now, and I will be idle. During the cold months, it is on you and your hunters that we will depend. Our houses will give us shelter but you must find us food. Each time you return home with a kill, you will be blessed, blessed even when food is plentiful, because meat is good and keeps us strong and builds our children into the strong men and women of tomorrow.'

Fiar sensed his ill-ease. Nobody equalled Sar when it came to building, but his skills did not extend to hunting, and when he had joined the hunters, he had proved a nuisance and a danger. He had great difficulty in keeping silent, and silence was essential. His loud voice had warned many an animal and caused the hunters to complain bitterly. Some were sure that he did it on purpose, especially when the prey was young. He did not have the heart for killing, and so the men did not want him with them. Fiar knew this. He knew too that since Sar would now have time on his hands, he would want to become a hunter again. Fiar searched frantically for a way out. Then he thought of the bear.

'Sar,' he said, 'we have fine shelter and we may not have a shortage of food during the winter, but we will be in danger from the bears in the cave when their food is scarce. They are our only enemy on this hill. Our children have been told not to go near the cave, but how long will they obey? How long before they provoke the bears? You know how my father's death has stayed with me. I am aware of the dangers in killing a bear. I need your help. I want you to build a cage strong enough to hold a grown bear, a cage that can withstand his enormous power, a cage that will ensure the safety of my hunters and rid us of the bears as well. None but you can do this work.'

Sar's mind raced, forming plans, rejecting and replacing designs. Suddenly, his houses looked better than before. He knew he would fulfil his second task as well as his first.

'I will begin on the morrow,' he replied simply.

They exchanged smiles. The rising smoke and the smell of good foods drifted up to them and called them back to the village.

Chapter 8

They had come to this new land well supplied and had prepared well for a harsh winter, so with their full larders and cosy houses they had no privations to suffer. Next year this land would have to feed them, but no one had any doubt that it could.

Each day the sun set lower in the sky. The tribe was anxious when the sun's decline continued and went much lower than it had in their old country. But Sen displayed no fear, so they were reassured.

The nights were very long and the days gave little opportunity for work. Even the hunters dared not roam too far in case the night should prevent their return. The skies were clear and this helped Sen in his calculations and observations. Since he spent much of his time standing out in the most exposed of places, he needed good protection. When wrapped in the warmest bear skins the tribe could offer, he looked like a woolly statue silhouetted against the rising sun of morning and the setting sun of evening.

A distant mountain was useful. The western side rose to a high peak, an unbroken ridge led out of it and spread into a high plateau on the south-eastern side. Each morning Sen watched as the sun rose over the central ridge. As the days grew shorter and colder, the sun began to peep through the gap between the ridge and the western peak first. This progression had to be marked down for future use, and the only way to record it was to mark the ground.

Sen chose an area of high, flat land to the west of the valley for his morning observations. He worked alone, unwilling to share his knowledge while he was still experimenting in this new land. First, he set a post in the centre of the space, driving it down into the ground until the top was level with his eye. This was to be his viewfinder and gnomon, so he had prepared it well. A bent twig formed a semi-circle on top. Nearby he stored a small pile of lighter posts, and a heavy stone maul with which to drive them into the ground. Each morning when the first rays of sunrise appeared over the mountain, Sen squinted through the bent twig on top of the centrepost and, having found a direct line on the rising sun, he drove a lighter post into the ground where it was touched by to the sun on that morning. Later, when the sun rose above the mountain and morning shadows appeared, the shadow cast by the gnomon would touch the marking post and Sen would know that his sighting had been correct on that morning. Each day the markers increased in number.

From the shore, Fer could see Sen at work. The posts were fanning out around the centrepost and, though he did not fully understand the formation, he knew that Sen's new knowledge would soon be put to use, for was not life a combination of earth and sun?

Other worries were occupying Fer. Now that the village had been built and the tribe was housed, he must concentrate on a bigger and more permanent structure: a house for the dead. This was indeed a healthy land, and no death had taken place yet. But as the days grew colder, death often came. He thought of Gar's lost family. It would be unlucky to have a strong male like Gar without a mate when spring came and the crops were sown again. Fertility of the land and the people was one. The women were nearly all heavy with life and would soon be giving birth. As the crops had been good, so the new-borns would be strong, and so the tribe would prosper. It was now time for giving birth so that the child would grow with the newly rising sun and be strong.

Fer hoped for another son this year, he already had one son and two daughters. Before planting time Gar must have a mate. When the days began to lengthen, as Sen assured him they would, he would send his hunters out to make contact with the other tribes who had lit fires.

By now the sun was high in the sky. Much time had passed, and the tasks of the day awaited him. Even Sen had left his markers and returned to the village. Fer turned back and found him sitting in the sun outside his house, contentedly picking meat from the carcass of a plump duck. He broke off a leg and passed it to Fer.

'The sun has moved from the gap to the peak and must now have reached the lowest point,' said Sen.

Fer looked puzzled.

'Look at the mountain,' Sen explained. 'This morning the sun rose above that peak, now it stays low in the sky, and it will set there,' with this he sketched the low arc of the sun across the sky with his hand.

'Sometimes I'm afraid that the sun will leave us and not return. You are sure?' asked Fer.

Sen pondered before replying. He hadn't intended making any announcement yet, but he knew Fer was voicing the fears of the whole tribe. Fer should be free of doubt. Besides, today was the first day that he was sure that life would go on because the shadow of the morning's sun did not require a new marker. From now on the markers would trace the return of the sun.

'I am quite sure,' he said to Fer. 'The low point has been reached. From now on the length of the day will increase, even though the weather will still be harsh and cold. That was the message of the morning sun, and I will be fully sure when I have checked the evening markers.'

Relief brightened Fer's eyes. He reached for another piece of duck and recalled hearing the old people speak of a time when the sun didn't shine and the earth froze over and nothing lived, a time when the sun went away. It was so long ago that no one knew whether this was a story or truth. But Sen had convinced him that this was not to happen and he was happy.

Sunset confirmed what sunrise had suggested. Sen spent some time watching the brilliant flaming sky and was over-awed. Such a display of glory demanded thanks and prayer, humbled and alone he felt the might and power about him. For years he had tried to understand this majestic power, this source of all things on earth. He had marked its track and felt its heat and seen it fill the land with plenty in its seasons, but he did not understand it and never could. He raised his voice and arms, and the sound washed across the waters and through the village, so that the tribe knew the good news and joined in the praise and was merry.

Finally, Sen prostrated himself on the now cold earth, linking both as it were. Just then the first star appeared, spluttering as if in difficulty, but growing steadier with oncoming darkness. Sen lay there until there were many stars in the sky and the chill of the earth began to seep through his bearskin. As he approached the village, he was not surprised to hear the cry of a new-born child.

Chapter 9

Confident now that spring would come and life could continue, the tribe tackled winter. The lake teemed with bird life and each day seemed to bring more. The great honking geese had come, and the hunters were using all sorts of stratagems to capture them. Often they hid for hours in the reeds, hoping that a flock would land close by. If one did, the hunters waited until they had settled down and then the attack was made. As soon as the first stones were thrown, the flock would rise with a thunderous beating of wings and wild agitated honking, annoyed by this new enemy.

Fiar soon became convinced that each flock had begun to place sentries, because the slightest stir in the reeds was often enough to alert the whole flock. He had trained his dog to retrieve the dead and injured geese gently, so as not to damage the flesh. Dogs were becoming more and more useful to man, although nature had not yet fully equipped them for the icy water on a winter's night.

When the snow came the land showed a new face, a face of gleaming, shimmering beauty. The lake was bluer than ever before, mirroring blue skies and snow-clad hills. Across the water the snow piled high on the bare forest floor and the leafless trees looked stark and cold. The hills were also covered, and each day much time was spent clearing snow to expose grass for the cattle and sheep. The goats had no difficulty as they nosed along the rockfaces, finding plenty to eat among the crannies and crevices.

It was a festive season of sorts as the children played and there was little work the parents could do. There was great disappointment on the morning that the thaw set in, and by evening only slight traces of snow remained in more sheltered places. But a further surprise was on the way. The weather grew bitterly cold, and every last bit of clothing was put to use. A biting wind blew for days, forcing them to huddle together by their fires. The children were cold and bad-tempered and their parents not much better. The men, especially, wanted to be out, but the cold prevented them, while the mothers did their best to shorten the long hours.

Yan was particularly good at telling tales and was much in demand. In those dark cold evenings, other children often slipped into the house in the hope that Yan would tell a story. Even Sar would listen with great interest. Often the same stories were repeated and the children joined in with the parts that they knew.

'A story! A story!' the children would chant and, gathering them around her, Yan would begin.

'The Brown Bear lived in the dark cave,' and straight away the whistling bitter wind and the cold were forgotten. 'He was a good bear, but he was lonely as nobody lived with him.'

'Just like Gar,' Saru chimed in.

'Winter came and the Brown Bear felt cold, so he moved further into the cave and rolled himself up tight and fell sound asleep. Water dripped from the roof of the cave on the lonely sleeping bear. He was all wet but didn't feel it, so sound was his sleep. Then the snow and frost came, and the water on his fur turned into ice.'

The little upturned faces became sad in the flickering firelight.

'The poor bear!' exclaimed a little girl.

'What happened, what happened?' Saru asked excitedly. And so the stories continued, holding the children enthralled.

The wind brought with it a black frost. The verges of

the lake froze, and then to everyone's amazement, ice covered the whole lake. The freezing conditions continued until the land and the lake became rock-hard, and the children woke shivering in the night and crying with cold. It was time to bring in some of the animals and their presence inside added much needed heat to each house.

The cold and hardship were tempered somewhat by wonder at what was happening about them. They had heard old stories of water turned to land but nobody had ever seen it before. Each day it became harder to break the ice to get the necessary water for human and animal needs. The children were the first to test it. They stepped on it gingerly, retreating at the sound of cracking, and then edging forth again. Soon they became more confident and began to run and play and slip and fall until their shouts of joy attracted their mothers' attention and they were ordered to shore. But the slaps and reprimands were soon forgotten and they returned to the ice as quickly as possible.

The frozen lake became a welcome distraction from the harsh weather and the problems of finding a food supply for the animals. Most of every day was spent searching in wooden areas for sheltered patches of withered grass and, when that became too difficult, stripping bark from trees for the cattle, for Fer had noticed that the goats had made it their main diet and were not lacking. But still the cattle became thinner, and their hungry mooing grew more plaintive by the day. This caused much anxiety, since cattle were to be the foundation of the new economy.

The island home had many advantages, but one of the greatest was the absence of wolves in a land where they roamed freely. It was comforting to know that the water was a barrier when their howls broke the stillness of the day and night. But when the lake and land became one, this protection was lost.

One evening, a ewe fell over a cliff and landed on her back among bushes at the base. Her pitiful bleating attracted the attention of a roaming pack of hungry wolves on the mainland. For a while they stood on the opposite bank, cautious about venturing onto the ice, but the attraction of easy food was strong. As if in reply to a snarl from the leader, they loped across the ice, and in moments they had torn the ewe apart, snarling and fighting one another for the hot flesh. The greater share went to the leader, a big she-wolf, heavy with pup.

Soon only some wool, blood and entrails marked the spot. Such easy prey was not to be ignored and, with more in prospect, the she-wolf led the pack up the hill. From the hilltop, she saw hungry cattle in the valley below. One cow, weak from hunger, had strayed away from the herd. She was an instant target. Stealthily the pack moved towards her and pounced. With a bellow of fear she turned to defend herself, but they sprang upon her. The she-wolf clamped her strong teeth on the throat. The cow's attempts to run were useless. She scarcely staggered three steps before she fell and was enveloped.

The herdsboys, meanwhile, were playing on the ice, slipping and sliding with shouts of laughter, oblivious to any danger, until the final terrified bellows of the dying cow sent fear through the air. The dogs barked, their hair bristling on their backs. The men ran to their homes for weapons. A chorus of unmistakable howls had confirmed their fears.

Chapter 10

Fer's son, Ferac, was the first to reach the house. He immediately took down the two strong bones which hung beside the door. He struck the great bones together, short clashes followed by a series of longer sounds. When the people heard the call they shuddered. This was the signal for serious danger. They dropped whatever they were doing and hastened towards Fer's house.

The village fires had burnt low. 'Stir the embers, fan the flames, much fire will be needed before this threat to us is removed,' Fer ordered, as he ran into the village. The people rushed to obey

Fer knew how savage a pack of hungry wolves could be. As if maddened by the taste of blood, they would continue to kill long after hunger had been satisfied. And they would attack humans without fear. If the pack was too big, then his hunters would not be able to overcome them. Other ways would have to be found to rid the island of this menace.

By now some of the cattle had returned, their eyes dilated with fear. But almost half the herd had not, terror had scattered them in all directions, and their bellows rang out. There were still two hours before sunset and many more cattle would die before dark gave some protection – some only, because those vicious creatures would hunt even in darkness.

There was no time to waste. Fiar and Gar would investigate the valley. This was dangerous and could be a costly strategy if the two best hunters were lost, but with so much cattle around, the wolves were unlikely to attack unless they crossed their path. Growls and snarls could be heard coming from the valley, so it seemed safe to go and look. The rest of the people had to round up as many cattle as possible and get them into the houses – a difficult task because of the excited condition of the terrified animals

Fer gathered the tribe around him and spoke quietly but firmly. 'The frozen water has not been our friend. It has allowed the wolves onto our island. We have every reason to be afraid, but we must stand together to overcome this terror.

'Fiar and Gar, go carefully and return quickly and safely. This duty we entrust to you, knowing that none is better suited to the task. The tribe glories in your great feats of the past and looks to the future and greater accomplishments.'

Fer placed a hand on the shoulder of each of his two hunters. Cre and Uish placed a hand on his shoulder, so that they stood in a formation somewhat similar in shape to an axehead. It had become a sign of unity and solidarity when a dangerous undertaking was about to commence.

Sen intoned the blessing: 'The leader gives strength to the heart of the power of the wedge. The broad end's strength is in the unity of purpose of loyal men. The front and back give strength to the heart. Take all our strength and courage with you. We call on the strength of the spirits of your lives past and your lives to come to go with you, lest your present strength should fail.'

Sen's words did not make sense to the others, but they knew their significance, their power and their ancient origin. The formation remained unmoving, while Sen spoke. The women and children watched for the slightest stir which might indicate weakness and give them reason for further fear. There was none.

When Fiar and Gar left, the village went straight to work. The women fed the fires, the bigger children helped by running to the piles of timber and dragging logs as big as their size and strength would allow. Alert to sudden danger, the mothers kept lookout, ready to bustle their young to Fer's house if wolves appeared over the brow of the hill, or came along the lakeshore in pursuit of the escaping cattle.

Meanwhile, the remaining men and youths collected the frightened cattle, speaking softly to them in an attempt to quieten the distressed creatures. Soon, what was left of the cattle population was housed. The pick of the herd was Gar's cow, given to him by Fer on their arrival. Beautiful but high-spirited, she refused to obey when her master's voice wasn't among those commanding her. When she ran terrified across the hill in full flight, all knew that she would not return.

The dogs had been tied inside the houses, they were no match for ravenous wolves. No attempt could be made to gather the sheep and goats. At least the goats could take shelter on the rocky mountain ledges, but the sheep had no protection against the rage of the marauding wolves and the loss would be great. However, human life was the main concern and fire was known to be the best protector, so Fer ordered fires to be built around the village. Nam and some of the women were helping.

'Quickly,' he ordered, in a harsh, concerned voice. If the wolves come to the village, and I think they will, you, Nam, will be in charge of the women and children. Gather them all into our home and stay there until the danger passes.'

Nam placed a hand on his shoulder. 'This danger will pass,' she assured him, though she wasn't convinced herself.

The main fires were burning fiercely now. Nam and the women took logs and started the new fires with them. Great care had to be taken in case a spark might set the thatched on fire. A strong wind could be disastrous. If the fires were too far apart and away from the houses, they would give no protection, and the pack would enter between them, if too near, there was a grave danger of inviting another enemy – fire – which would be just as difficult to handle. Fer consulted with Sen and came to a decision. Instead of a circle the fire barrier would be U-shaped, close to the houses on the east and north, far out on the west, while the two legs would stretch down to the water's edge. The tribe worked feverishly to obey his order.

Luckily the weather had been somewhat milder that day, and Sen had predicted an end to the great frost. Since the black winds that heralded the freezing conditions had ceased, there had been no wind of any consequence, but the air was stirring again and wisps of clouds were drifting in from the west.

Meanwhile, Fiar and Gar had reached the Eagles' Rock. They had moved stealthily, avoiding open spaces, and their approach had taken them to the craggier northern face of the island hill. They knew well the danger of encountering the pack in an open area. Gar's concentration and attention had wavered when he saw his cow charging across the hill. Only Fiar's firm restraining hand on his shoulder had held him in check.

'No, Gar, we have a job to do. She might yet turn back to safety,' Fiar whispered, but without conviction. The likely loss of his only cow, his most valuable possession, added a sickening dimension to Gar's fear.

Lying flat on the rock, they looked down into the valley and were aghast. A scene of savagery and slaughter lay beneath them. Strewn remains of three cattle and perhaps five sheep – it was difficult to be sure – their blood, flesh, bones, wool and skins, lay scattered in all directions. The savage wolves were still tearing and snarling, their shaggy winter coats blanketed in blood. Satiated with the warm flesh and the victory of the kill, they no longer fought each other for a share. There was more than enough for all, but the growling and snarling went on in continual warning. Twenty-three, twenty-four, twenty-five ... the dismayed watchers counted.

The she-wolf had eaten enough and withdrew to sit a little further up the slope. She sat and licked at her blood-spattered coat. Her stomach, swollen with her ripe litter, was distended and her milk-filled nipples showed full. She yawned and lay on her side to rest but kept an eye on the pack below. It was a signal to the others to rest also, and they began to leave the torn carcasses.

Just then a frightened bellow sounded. Gar's cow was running up the hill close to the resting she-wolf. In a second, the she-wolf was up. She gave a howl of command, and the pack swung up the hill in full pursuit. Gar and Fiar stared in horror. The wolves split into two groups. They would attack from both sides. They had much more speed on the hill and she was quickly overtaken. A strong male sunk his teeth in just above the hock. He was dragged along by the fleeing cow. Two others struck from the front. She was forced to stop.

Now her bellows signalled fear and rage. She was surrounded, but she butted and kicked. When one leapt onto her back, she swung around with such speed that she cast him from her again. Plunging her horn into the side of another, she crushed his ribs and, when he fell to the ground, she trampled him to death. The same horn caught another in the mouth, ripping teeth and bone and sending him yelping away. But there were too many of them. The she-wolf waited her moment, and then sank her teeth into the weakening animal's throat. It was over.

Gar sobbed. His cow had fought alone, killing or disabling five of the pack. And as he watched, her stomach was ripped open and a wolf dragged out a well-developed calf. It was dead. He swore revenge.

The sun had set and it was a dull twilight with no hint of the crisp sparkle of frost. Fiar tugged at Gar to leave, but he remained transfixed.

'Come on, Gar,' Fiar urged. 'We must get back to the village. They need us, we must tell them how many there are. Come now, you can do nothing for her.'

He turned away reluctantly, but not before he saw the she-wolf command the pack away from his brave dead cow, and, using the carcass for shelter, lie out on the ground to give birth to the first of her litter.

'They will not leave this island alive,' Gar swore, as they headed for the village with heavy hearts and bad news.

Chapter 11

Great rain-clouds gathered in the west, and the night grew milder. The thaw had begun, and already a thin film of water covered the ice. Sen had been down at the water's edge and hurried back to Fer.

'The ice is melting,' he said. 'Our problem will be more serious still if the wolf-pack don't have a way of recrossing to the mainland.'

Fer sighed. 'I wish Fiar and Gar would return. They are long overdue. What can be delaying them?'

At last Cre saw them approaching. Before a word had been spoken, their shocked condition was obvious. Gar was pale and trembling. Fer led them to his house, where he took out a precious skin of wine. They drank deeply. It was Fiar who recounted what they had witnessed – the slaughter in the valley, the ferocity of the she-wolf and the brave death of Gar's cow.

'She has reduced the pack by five at least,' Fiar concluded.

While Gar listened, the final scene on the hill kept flashing through his mind with frightening clarity, and each bloody lunge exploded in his mind again and again. Tonight, when every man was needed, Gar would stay inside and sleep – it was clear that in his present condition his actions could not be depended on to be rational. Fer feared that when the wolves came, Gar would expose himself to the danger of a death similar to that of his cow's.

'You must take rest, Gar. Go with Sen. Rest! You will be needed later.' Fer's command was gentle and Gar knew that he must obey. Reluctantly, he followed Sen to his house. He refused food, but drank the wine offered. Soon it began to take effect and he lay down.

'Wolves are evil. They take all they can,' Sen said softly.

'The sea took my family, my animals and all my possessions. Now the wolves have taken my cow. I cannot take revenge on the sea, but the wolves will feel my axe and arrows,' Gar answered with choked hurt.

As he sat watching him, Sen could hear Gar's sobs until deep sleep blurred the reality.

* * *

Discipline and order are very important for survival, Fer thought, and his people had been well tested – leaving their homeland, the hazardous sea-crossing, the search for the new home – all had held dangers that were overcome by their unshakable unity and loyalty to him. Fer had no doubt that they would confront this challenge, possibly their greatest challenge, and conquer it. No wolf pack could deprive them of their life here. Many generations would grow strong in this good land, strong in numbers and prosperity.

All the women and children were now safely in Fer's house, which was furthest from the perimeter of the village and the last line if outer defences failed. The cattle had been left unattended in the other houses. It was safer. If the wolves came, the occupants could be trampled by the panicking cattle. Protecting his people's lives was the most important thing. Fer saw no fear on the women's faces. Instead the firelight showed a solid determination in their eyes, and they had passed this calmness on to their children. The only sound in the large room was the crackling of flames and an occasional whimper from a sleeping child. The dogs were lying alert and tense. Unused to being confined, they bristled, but lay down again on seeing Fer.

'The pack is strong and fierce,' Fer began, addressing the women and children, 'and already we have suffered loss, but we have been spared the loss of human life. Feel safe tonight. The fires are blazing and our men keep watch and are ready for any attack. So take your rest, for tomorrow we will need strength and courage. Ask for strength and courage for your men and be ready to help them with your own. We will succeed.'

He turned and left to move among the men on watch between the fires, speaking briefly with each and arranging periods of rest, so that they too could conserve some energy for the long tomorrow. He passed Sen's house to check on Gar and, satisfied, he returned to the line of fires, to take his place in the watch and maintain the fires. He carried two axes stuck in his belt and a spear in his right hand. He stuck the handle of the spear in the ground with some difficulty, rubbed his hands together and stood closer to a fire.

Dusk had changed to dark night. The frosty air had been dispelled but a coldness still rose from the solid ground. Fer shivered. He knew that fear not cold was the real cause of the shiver. With so much heat about, he thought, how could one be cold? Though Fer might feel fear like another, he could not be seen to show it, so he stood and thought and hoped. He piled on more logs and, when the heat became too much to bear, moved away towards the next fire.

Away from the crackling sounds, he could hear the night calls of the many birds. They knew that the thaw had come and were not concerned with sleep. They had managed to keep an area of water open for themselves all though the great frost, which though not large enough to accommodate all of them, was at least a help. He was glad that he had made the young boys break other small shore areas for the weaker birds each morning. His spirits plummeted when he thought of the birds' plight, but he checked himself quickly. He could not allow himself a moment's despair, nor could he doubt the enormity of the task that the morning would bring. Unity of movement and purpose would be vital. The tribe must stay together, no matter what. The children could not be left alone, nor could he spare any men to stay behind and protect them. There were few enough of them as it was. The odds were only slightly in their favour. But the fires could save them.

He was warm now. The strong skins which wrapped his feet and legs, his warm tunic, the sheepskin across his shoulders, and the cowl of deerskin, were more than adequate for the milder weather, and so he stayed away from the fires, going to them only when stoking was needed. Little by little a plan took shape. He would discuss it with the others in the morning, but he felt sure that they would agree. Satisfied that he had reached a good decision, he relaxed, and a tiredness came on him. He stretched himself and walked to the nearest house where a jar of water stood outside the door. He poured water into his cupped hands and drank. Then he splashed water on his face and felt refreshed. Turning towards the house to relieve himself, he heard the dogs stir inside the house, and then growl. He looked about quickly, but saw nothing to cause alarm.

'Can you see anything?' he called across to Cre.

'No. But they must be coming this way. The dogs are agitated. We should call the others.'

Fer hesitated, not wanting to cause unnecessary panic, but the barking and growling had increased, and the cattle were bellowing in renewed fear. It was time to assemble the men and some of the stronger youths who could stand and fight. He strode over to where he had left the bones, raised them and struck them loudly together. The sound echoed across the hills, startling the bird-life. Immediately the men were at their posts. Each person was armed with a long blazing torch picked from the fires. They were ready.

The wolf pack moved stealthily down the hill, approaching the village from the east, and stopped some distance from the fires. The sounds of dogs and cattle called to them, but the fires posed problems. Fer, Cre and Sar stood in the gaps between the fires on that side, waiting for them. Keeping a safe distance from the flames, the pack circled the line of fires searching for a weak spot. An attack was imminent.

Fer shouted and the first part of the strategy began. The defenders shouted as loudly as they could, making the most ferocious sounds and all the time swinging the flaming torches in wide circles. A pile of stones was heaped beside each man. Grabbing a handful, the men loosed a barrage at the stunned pack. Some stones struck home and a few wolves went yelping away. One lay twitching on the ground and would not rise again. The pack retreated, their teeth bared and angry eyes flashing in the reflected flames. And then they attacked, heading for the widest gap between the fires where at that moment only Sar stood. As the pack swept down on him, he shouted for help. He didn't see the wolf coming from his left side until it leaped and dug its teeth into his shoulder, knocking him to the ground. Gar, who had been woken by the yelling, sped to Sar's aid. He crashed his axe down on the wolf's skull with such force that it burst open and the wolf fell dead.

'For my cow,' he roared, and were it not for Sar he would have given chase. The others raced up to counter the attack with their torches. Blood gushed from Sar's torn shoulder. Gar carried him across to Fer's house, shouting at the women to open up and tend the wounded man.

Quietly Nam said to Yan, 'Outside under the eaves, the spiders live. Go and gather some web to stanch the wound. Ish, warm up the contents of that jar. It will heal the wound quickly and safely.'

The children strained to see what Nam was doing. Sar's injury was a welcome distraction, and they watched his face closely.

The cobwebs were very effective, and before long Nam had prepared a concoction of oak bark and crushed garlic which she used as a poultice on the shoulder, covering it with broad dock leaves. She then strapped Sar's arm tightly to his chest. All the while she was crooning softly as a mother would soothe her child to sleep, but the words were a mantra of cure.

'It will soon be well,' she said, as she finished. Sar nodded grimly and spoke his thanks.

When Gar returned to the fires, the men were shocked and frightened. Even fire might not keep the vicious creatures away, and Sar's scream of terror still rang in their ears. They stood waiting. Where would the next attack come from? Just then a piercing howl was heard from the hilltop, a howl that blotted out all other sound. The pack turned and without a moment's hesitation, loped up the hillside and away. The she-wolf had called. The attack was over, at least for the present.

'If we fail to drive them off the island tomorrow, we will have to leave ourselves,' Fer announced.

'It will be very difficult, but we must succeed before the ice melts. It must be done tomorrow,' Fiar said with determination.

There was silence while each man collected his thoughts. Then Fer spoke. 'We must succeed, and we will. We must drive them off the hill by sweeping along its width. To do that we'll need everybody to form the line.'

'Even then will we have enough people?' asked Uish.

'Not enough, but we must do the best we can,' replied Fer. 'The women and children can be part of the line and will stay between the men. They will be vital to success.'

'What do you mean?' asked Uish.

'They won't have weapons,' answered Fer, 'but they will have bones and will make as much noise as possible. If fire is the weapon of the night, then sound is the weapon of the day. We will carry our hunting tools and fight to the death if necessary.'

'If it comes to a fight,' said Gar, 'it will be a fight to the end.'

Fer knew that nothing else could be done. There was no other way and the plan was quickly agreed on. The spirits of their past lives would strengthen them.

'We will be ready to move at first light,' Fer said. 'Some must keep watch now, but the others must seek rest and prepare for morning. Do not enter your homes if there are cattle within, but find shelter any place you can. In the morning we will not wait for food, so eat now and be strong. We will succeed because we must.'

As they dispersed, the first drops of rain began to fall. Fer hoped the thaw would not come too soon.

* * *

Grey morning broke and soft rain driven by a light breeze fell. It could have been any mild winter's morning. But this morning was different. The silence spoke loudest as each person's thoughts dwelt on the encounter ahead. Scouts brought back the news that the pack had not gone to the western side of the village. The drive could begin out from the valley and, as the island narrowed, it might just be possible to prevent the pack from turning back and breaking through the line and getting to the unprotected village. Before setting off, Sen chanted aloud, seeking help from the gods and raising the people's flagging spirits by assuring them that they would succeed.

A line was formed across the brow of the hill and Fer gave the signal to move forward. Saru made sure that he was next to Isht. She smiled when she saw him.

'I'll mind you,' she joked. For Isht this was a great adventure and she would play her part fully.

The sight of the dead animals had depressed the villagers, but it gave way to a determination to extract revenge. The dogs strained at their leashes. They would not be let loose unless the pack attacked. The beat of the bones was slow at first, slow and ominous and heavy on the air. It was loud and regular and seemed to echo the frightened heartbeat of the beaters. On they went, past what remained of Gar's cow, and up to the hilltop where the celebratory fire had blazed. Now the descent began and the encounter came nearer. The rhythm of the bones increased in pace and volume. A sweat of fear glistened on their foreheads and their hands were clammy. As the island narrowed, the line drew closer and this closeness brought comfort.

They had reached the bottom of the hill. Not a single wolf. They turned to each other in disbelief. Perhaps the pack had somehow avoided the line and managed to move to the western side of the island. But this was impossible. Relief set in. The pack must have crossed the ice-bridge. That chilling howl of the she-wolf must have been the command to leave. She needed to take her new litter away from danger. Weeping, the women hugged their children, while the men spoke with raised voices and retold the adventures of the night before. Saru was sent back with the good news to the injured Sar who was waiting anxiously in his house. Isht went with him. They held hands for a moment on the hilltop and gazed in awe at the slaughter. They stopped to look at the remains of a big wolf, a victim of Gar's cow. Its fangs were bared in death.

'We should have killed them all,' Saru said.

'Take out those two strong fangs with your axe,' Isht demanded. 'We'll hang one each from our necks. It'll be our bond and a pledge to kill wolves whenever we can.'

Chapter 12

The little white flowers announced that growth had begun again, and the days stretched and were milder. The earth began to call, and the tribe inspected their jars of seed regularly to make sure their contents were ready to grow and yield in plenty. Their eyes lingered on the jars as if to coax growth within. They imagined seasons to come, with fields waving green in the summer breeze, and the gold of autumn harvest.

But it was not yet the day for cultivation or planting. There was an order that must be followed. Fer would tell them when Sen was sure that the sun was calling. His pattern of sun-marking stakes fanned out over a large area now, as the sun continued to rise higher each day. Preparations were well advanced, tools and seeds were ready, and so was an eagerness on the part of the tribe to test this promising land. Soon ... soon ...

Nature had taken its own course and the young animals were being born. Because the herds had been decimated by the wolves, each birth was vital and received the very best of care and attention all day and all night. As the nights were still long, the givers of birth were housed inside where their birth pains and struggles were shared and assisted by the family. Even with all that care, there were losses and each loss weighed heavy when added to the previous losses. Still, the spring birthing was deemed satisfactory, and calves, lambs and kids were afforded the pride of place that their contribution to the future prosperity of the tribe deserved. Fresh milk was plentiful now, and this valuable liquid gave strength and energy to young and old, and so the tribe prepared itself for the work ahead.

Fer still resolved that Gar should have a mate for

spring. Yet he hesitated to send his hunters to the nearest habitation from which smoke rose constantly. Sometimes smoke drifted up from places in the forest, but this indicated only a hunter's camp. As yet his hunters hadn't had to travel far as game had been abundant about the lake. Soon they would have to venture out further.

Gar was impatient for this. Although he was a man almost without property, he knew that he could depend on Fer and his friends to provide him with possessions and, if he were lucky, his new woman might bring some goods with her too. Days went by, and his impatience grew, but still Fer waited. His instinct told him to wait, and Sen agreed.

'I have seen signs that Gar will not be long alone. Each sign carries a caution which says that she will come to him. It says not to seek, but to wait, and the signs become clearer daily. I know that soon she will come,' Sen confided to Fer.

Fer said nothing of this to Gar. And still the days passed, and the time to begin work drew nearer and Gar became despondent, then dour and irascible. And Fer waited and started to doubt both his instinct and Sen's prediction. The planting had to be completed by the time night and day were once again the same length. Tomorrow the work would have to begin and then even hunting would take second place. The hunters had brought in a stock which would last for many days. Much had been cooked, and some had been covered in mud and buried deep in the boggy margins of the lake where it would remain fresh for quite a long time.

Fer gave the order to commence work. The morning broke clear and bright. Soft clouds were driven across the sky by the light breezes. The usual cold winds of this time of year had not as yet come, and it was hoped that the seeds would be safe in the ground when the cold spell came. There was a flurry of activity all about.

The planting enclosures were simple and mostly of equal size. A simple fence of uprights with twigs woven in between had been prepared to keep out the animals when growth began. During part of the winter, the animals had been penned up at night. Their sharp hooves had crushed the remaining grass into the ground, and their manure would be a help to growth. Using pointed saplings, the people had scratched the remaining grass from the ground and exposed the brown earth to the frost and snow to let air at the soil.

Now in spring, the saplings were again put to use. The ground was pierced and scored over and over until the fresh rich soil, soft and fine to the touch, marked the hillside, and awaited the plantings. Mother Earth was giving her great gift freely and the returns would be generous. Men and women toiled happily, and the children helped, doing as their parents did once the first hard breaking had been done. They picked out stones and gathered them in small heaps to be disposed of later, and if the shape of any suggested other use it was put aside carefully.

The least enthusiastic worker was Gar, alone in his patch on the slope of the hill. His needs were few and so his patch was smaller than the rest. Fer had mentioned sending the hunters to find somebody for him. This had not happened. Hurt, angry and alone, Gar vowed that he would go and find himself a female companion. He could not and would not wait any longer. He worked, but his mind was elsewhere. He knew the direction to take, and his desire easily overcame his fear of the forest. He would mark his path clearly and could then return when he wished. But he would not return alone. Dreams filled his head. She was young and beautiful. Her brown hair fell on her shoulders and her gentle eyes laughed as hand in hand they ran on the hill. He knew that this was love, and his heart swelled in his breast so that he raised a great shout.

Uish watched, then approached Gar as the shout and raised arms subsided into a man with stooped shoulders standing alone. Uish understood and was sorry for Gar. His greeting startled Gar from his pleasant reverie, but, seeing a friend, Gar was glad and he raised his hand in welcome.

'I came to see how your work was going, Gar,' Uish said.

'As you see, Uish, not very well, but I'll get enough done for my own needs and that won't take much effort,' Gar replied. 'You've much work to do, Uish, but your family can help you, here it is hard to work alone and with little purpose.'

They were good friends and Gar held no secrets from Uish. 'I don't want to be alone any longer,' he continued, 'but Fer does not seem to understand. I refuse to wait any longer. I'm going to go from here and find a companion, even if I have to travel far and farther still.'

Angrily he hurled the sapling at the ground. It sank deep into the earth. The muscles rippled on his strong arms and he stood with feet apart and head bowed. Uish slapped his hand on Gar's shoulder, and they both sat down on the hillside. Below them the lake sparkled in the sunshine.

'When the planting is over, I'll go with you,' Uish offered.

Their friendship demanded this offer, but Uish knew that Gar would not take him from his family, even for a short while.

They stared across the lake in silence. Little puffs of smoke could be seen wafting up from the nearest settlement. Ignoring Uish's offer, even though it would remain in his mind, Gar pointed and said, 'I know that I must go there and that I will find there the companion I need. Uish, I have seen her in dreams and I must go.'

Uish understood. Uish had brought a small jar, perfectly made as only a very skilled person could do. A pattern of lines adorned the belly of the jar and an unusual marking decorated the lip on top. It was a gift to Gar from Uish and his family and contained a small amount of precious seed, which they could scarcely do without, but Gar was in need and must be helped. Gar was grateful. This was the first gift. There would be others, but this would remain the most prized. He thanked Uish and thanked him also for coming when he did. He had needed a friend and, having spoken to Uish, he was now certain of the course that lay ahead.

A shout interrupted the tribe's labours. Everyone turned to look across the lake to the south from where the human voice had sounded. A voice! People! Strangers! The voice called again. There on the shore stood three people and, as the words floated clearly across the water, everyone knew that they were calling to be brought across to the island.

The tribe rushed to the shore. Fer nodded to Sar whose fine boat was on the water and ready to sail. It would carry Sar and the three easily. There was a buzz of excited chatter as the boat crossed the calm waters and approached the other shore, and then all became quiet. Something was happening. Something of great importance.

The tribe strained to see the new arrivals. As the boat drew nearer, they saw that they looked not unlike themselves. Their dress was similar, though brighter and they wore many ornaments. A dog barked and set off a chorus of growls. To them strangers were not welcome.

Gar realised that the three were men. He had hoped that one might be a woman. But he felt sure that they could tell him where he had to go. His mind filled with questions. The boat touched shore, the visitors disembarked.

Chapter 13

His name was Arg, and he had travelled far. He had crossed many lands and many seas and had brought many good things to trade and much news, news of happenings and news of progress. His visit was most welcome.

His two companions, or servants, had been with him for a long time. They were twins. Both deaf and dumb, their disability had led the head-man of their tribe to trade them to Arg when they were about eight summers old. Their parents' lamentations availed nothing, but Arg promised them that he would take good care of them and this he had done. They understood each other well, master and servants, and an elaborate set of signs made communication possible among them. Arg referred to both as 'Them', never having needed to name them, but for each he had a separate hand-sign, though one was seldom without the other. Even now, as Arg sat on Fer's right-hand side at the camp-fire, they stood straight across from him, a little removed, but on the alert to his needs or requests.

Excitement pervaded the village. They felt as if they were on public display for the first time. The women hastily tidied themselves, while the men stood taller as if competing with the newly-arrived males. Even the children caught the mood of feverish anticipation.

Once welcome had been extended, it was proper that hospitality should be given. Food was prepared while Arg went to Fer's house to rest and share the very last of the wine. Sen joined them there and, after a short consultation, Fer announced that the day's work was over, that no trading would be done until the morrow and that the whole tribe would feast with the visitors.

Delighted, everyone returned home to prepare a contribution to the feast. Although each household had a supply of cooked meat, this occasion demanded freshly cooked meat. It was a sign of hospitality. The young girls mixed flour, which the boys had ground on quern stones, with water. Larger stones were placed within the fires to heat.

Soon they were red hot, and, standing above the flames, they formed a platform oven on which the cakes could be baked. Delicious juices from the meat cooking above them trickled down and added much to the taste. Eggs were collected from nests and young watercress, sorrel and herbs from the hillside added flavour to the rich meal. It was only on such rare festive occasions that the women, children and men were permitted to dine together as a community.

It was a memorable feast, and it lifted the tribe's spirits after the trials and deprivations of winter. Arg took out a skin of wine, which passed from person to person and was consumed with much jostling and jollity. When everyone had eaten and drunk to their satisfaction, Arg became the focal point. The tribe gathered around the central fire to hear him speak of his travels. But first the children, complaining bitterly, were sent away. Only the male youths were allowed to stay. They would hear news of the world outside their island home and this was important knowledge.

Arg's hair was grey and his face wrinkled. He looked old, but his quick decisive movements suggested otherwise. Though small and slightly stooped, there was a spring in his step, and his bones carried no aches to slow his rapid progress. He wore brightly coloured beads around his neck and wrists and a band of purple cloth around his head that was very distinctive. His clothes were of plain undyed wool, except for his cloth cloak which was red and yellow, colours which to the eyes of those gathered around were usually found only in nature at differing times of the year. Arg's voice also impressed. It carried a gravity which demanded attention, and the watchers hoped that he would teach them his secrets.

'I have travelled far, but as yet have never seen a place as lovely as your home,' he began. 'Your land is rich and will yield in plenty to make you prosperous, and your lake gives you pure water, food and protection. Trees do not encroach on your land, and so the soil cries out for seed and will produce sturdy crops and make you a strong race. The gods who led you here had a great concern for you.

'But you are not alone in this fair land. Many live near the coast and many have moved inland to where the water is. The lakes and rivers welcome people and animals. Man is clearing the forests and, like you, has learnt to glean a good living from the land. Some of the coastal dwellers are only now learning your skills. Some are slow to understand and change, but the time of great change is here and is good for all.'

Gar wanted to ask where these other people lived, but Cre, anticipating his intention, nudged him and he restrained himself.

Arg continued: 'The great changes come from the east, with the rising sun, brightening the world as does the morning sun. New types of seed produce great harvests, new vines yield grapes richer in wine. There are new and better ways of making cloth thicker and warmer and using colour to make it more beautiful. These things I see as I travel and I bring with me from land to land and from tribe to tribe. Some I bring to you. Some only, because you are new to this land and have brought new ways with you.'

Here he paused, watching for a reaction. Fer nodded, and so he continued. 'Milk is the best of food and can be made to last longer. There are better ways of keeping meat fresh and preserving fruit. I have new cures for sickness, using plants and berries. Now a man can live for thirty-five summers and women who give birth without difficulty can also grow old with their men. Now, not as many of your children need die before they become true members of the tribe. If you listen to what I have to tell you, your tribe will gain and increase in number and strength.'

Arg knew the tribe was listening spellbound. He stopped speaking and a buzz of conversation broke out. He wasn't in any great hurry now. These people wanted what he was offering and he would be well rewarded, but then so would they. In every mind tradeable commodities were being listed. Each man hoped that he would have enough to get what he needed. Each woman hoped that Arg had brought some clothes dyes. They had long envied the splendid plumage of the birds and the various shades of the animal kingdom. Only Gar was uninterested in material things, though he had a good supply of hides to trade. There was just one thing that Gar wanted – but he would have to wait until an opportunity presented itself, then he would question Arg.

Arg's servants had been watching intently and waiting for the signal, a simple nod of the head from Arg, to come forward with a large pack made of deerskin. They placed it before Arg who opened it carefully. Putting his hand inside, he drew out a magnificent axe. It seemed to glitter in the flames. The blade was wider than a man's hand and was made of shining black stone which had been ground down to a perfect edge. Even the hafting was more substantial than that which Uish did so well.

Its maker had bored the wide and sturdy wooden handle, inserted the narrow end of the blade through it and bound it tightly with thongs. It was simple – so simple!

Uish gave a gasp of wonder and coming forward extended both hands. Arg placed the splendid tool in his hands, and Uish spent a long minute unmoving, gazing at it, his mind racing with thoughts of producing axes just as perfect.

Uish reluctantly returned the axe. Arg put it back in the pack and withdrew a maul for quarry work, some finely ground flint knives, bones, pins and combs, delicately shaped bone fish-hooks, bracelets and necklaces of shell and stone, in red and blue and green and white and mixtures of every shade under the sun. Now it was the women's turn to gasp.

Arg had shown enough and he knew that the trade would be good. He returned everything to the pack quietly and motioned to the twins to take it away. Fer, as interested as any and as disappointed to see the objects being removed, knew that the day's end had come and it was rest time.

'Go to your homes,' Fer said. 'Tomorrow might be a trade day, but there is much work to be done. If Arg would consent to stay, we could complete our planting before we trade. We would know then if we have surplus grain to trade and, while we are planting, Arg could visit and trade some of the new seed he carries. During that time he might teach us some of his skills.'

Arg nodded his assent, and the people began to leave for home, though not entirely happily – the end of the planting seemed a long way off.

Soon only Arg, Fer and Sen remained by the fireside with the twins standing inconspicuously in the background. Gar had bided his time, but now he approached the fire and sat.

'Arg, I am without a woman,' he began. 'I need your help and advice. In your travels you must have come upon settlements with girls of child-bearing years. Tell me where I can find one such and I'll set out at first light to seek her and bring her home. I have seen her in dreams. I know her. I have only to find her. You can tell me where to go.'

The moon appeared from behind the clouds and shone on the lake. Arg gazed across the water and a brightness filled his eye, not a reflection of fire or moon, but a memory of a time long past when he too had lost the mate of his youth and was lonely. He was happy for Gar, happy that he could help him and happy that the girl at the last settlement he had visited was so suitable. She would be pleased to live here with Gar, who seemed a good man. And yet the thought brought sadness too and the brightness was misted over. Alone he would have cried for what had been, but not now, with Gar watching so intently, with so much expectation.

He shrugged his shoulders. 'Gar, I have seen her too, and not long ago. She is as lovely as your dreams of her, and she is waiting for you.'

He paused, took a tiny arrow-head from his pocket and looked at it thoughtfully. 'Her father gave me this to give to the man that I would choose for her. I haven't travelled far and already I seem to have found a likely companion for her. But I must be sure because I am indebted to her also. I was ill while I was with her people, and it was her good care and kindness that restored me to health.'

Turning to the others, he asked, 'Is there any reason why I should look further?'

Sen replied, 'Gar's only fault is that he has little property. He has suffered much loss and has no herd. But the tribe will help him, we are all in his debt for many reasons. What property is expected? The tribe will fulfil whatever is demanded.

'And it must also be remembered that he is next to Fer in rank. He knows farming better than most and is a skilled hunter. She would be well cared for. We know, we have seen him with a family before now.'

'You are most convincing, Sen,' Arg replied. 'It seems that I have found the right man. Property is not as important as the right man. Her father was clear about this. He will gladly send good stock to the right man and you, Gar, are that man.' He handed Gar the arrow-head.

Arg then handed Gar a beautiful blue bracelet and said: 'You will not go to her but you will send her this gift. She lives two days in that direction.' He pointed southwards across the lake to where smoke was often seen.

'My servants will carry the arrow-head and the bracelet to her. Your message will be understood and, when the planting is over, she and her people will come. On the spring festival you will become one. Her name is Deir.'

Chapter 14

Work continued in the fields, but now there was an air of anticipation and excitement as the end was in sight, and there would be a celebration. Everyday activities seemed to hold more purpose. Perhaps this was partly in an effort to impress Arg, who would spread news to other tribes that they were an industrious people, improving their trade outside their island home.

Arg's arrival had ended their isolation. The distant wisps of smoke had an identity now, as Arg could point to the distance and tell them who lived there and there. Many tribes were still on the move, Arg explained, planting very little, rearing some stock, but mainly relying on hunting and what they could gather from the earth. Most of them stayed by the great rivers and the sea. Fer's people had brought many new ideas with them which would be the envy of many of the natives, Arg thought, but he was slow to say this – he had things to trade. For instance, the new seed he had brought from across the seas was superior to that which the tribe was planting. Fer had decided to acquire some and plant it in common ground. The yield would be retained for distribution to individuals in the coming year.

Already Gar's life had changed. Now that the twins had left with his message, he was happy. Gone was the despair and lethargy with which he had approached his work. Now, no task seemed to be too great and his skills, which he had chosen to forget, were in use again. His soil seemed the most fertile in the village, almost as if it were under command to produce more. His life now had purpose, and as he worked he dreamed. Often Gar worked on long after all the others had stopped, until somebody came to tell him of day's end, or called him to join in the evening meal. The tribe was pleased for Gar and hoped that his new woman would be all that Arg had promised.

Uish's life had changed since the night of Arg's arrival too, when he held the black axe for the first time. When the tribe had acquired it he was ecstatic. Too fine for anything but ceremonial use, it would remain a prestigious tribal possession for many generations. Uish was a master craftsman, he had perfected his father's teaching and improved long-established techniques. But never had he ground an axe to such smoothness, found an axe with the balance of the black axe, never had he succeeded in honing one to the sharpness of that axe. The hafting was so simple and secure, he mused, why hadn't he thought of it himself? He was taken aback when he compared his own clumsy method. He hoped to reproduce it successfully. Fer put the axe in his care, knowing that it could not be in better hands.

But there was a problem! He could not find the same black stone on the island and hills. The nodules of black stone, bedded in the soft rock in the valley, were small and difficult to work.

'Where does the good black stone come from?' he asked Arg one evening.

Pointing north, Arg replied, 'Far away, many days away, around the coast and to the place where the land ends. There is plenty of black stone there, and many axes are made and traded far and wide.'

'How can I get there?' Uish wanted to know, his mind full of dreams.

'It's too far away.' Arg's reply was just what Uish didn't want to hear. 'Use the material you have here and eventually you will make implements just as fine.'

But Uish knew that this was not so, though he would try. But in his dreams he would always see the land of the black stone and wish to be there to make an axe as perfect as the black axe. He held it in his hand and felt a power from it coursing through his veins. The time for admiration was over. He must begin work. He felt as excited as when he had first succeeded in flaking an arrow-head and making an axe.

If Arg had stayed for only a day or two, as he had first intended, the tribe would have rushed to acquire some of his desirable goods, but when it became known that he would be with them until after the spring festival, the people began to assess their tradeable goods. Many found that they possessed things which could be done without. Two or three such objects could be traded wisely for one essential object. So trading continued each day and a complicated barter system developed, as the people traded first among themselves for what they needed to trade with Arg, then with Arg for what had become to them an essential.

Arg missed his servants. He had grown unused to doing anything for himself, but there were plenty of willing helpers available, and though he was engaged in business and accumulating a satisfactory profit, he was still a guest of the tribe and received generous food and comfortable shelter. In fact, the thought had crossed his mind that to remain here would not be a bad idea. But he knew that the call of other places was too strong. He promised himself however, that when his journeys were over, he would come back here to the peace and quiet and contentment of being with good people.

By day, the children followed Arg everywhere. To them he represented another world, a world of colour and bright things. He liked the children and being a natural storyteller, was always ready to stop his dealings and sit with them and tell of his wonderful adventures. They heard of distant lands where people spoke in different tongues, lands so far from the sea that it took seasons to reach them, where the summers were unbearably hot and the winters freezing cold. But it was his stories of spirits and strange happenings which really thrilled his young audience and caused sleepless nights – and angry parents. Never were their chores done so quickly, as they rushed to be with Arg again. Generally though, their parents were pleased that Arg was so willing to be with the children. This was an education for them and much of what they learnt would be of benefit to them.

At night, when the evening meal was over and the sun had set, it was the adults' turn to hear his tales and they listened just as carefully, especially when he spoke of other settlements in their new land.

'Do all the people in this land treat their dead as we do?' Sen asked one evening.

Arg paused and then replied, 'I notice that you have not built a burial chamber yet. Is it your intention to change from the practices of your forebears?'

'While our crops are growing, we will build the chamber. We have had no time to spare so far. The gods have been kind, and no adult life has been taken yet. We hope it will be so until the chamber is ready to receive them. As you know, we bury our children in the earth and they are recreated without the greater powers of earth and sun. They are recalled solely by man and woman. But even they were born strong this year and all have survived,' explained Fer.

The stars shone brightly, and the flames and sparks rising from the fire seemed to link the sky and earth, giving greater meaning to their talk, as they believed that the bright lights of the sky were the temporary dwelling-places of the dead. They lived among the stars and were reincarnated through the power of sun and earth working through man and woman.

'Some tribes I've visited think it necessary to sacrifice their first-born, but this practice is cruel and weakens the tribe. The wisest know and have spoken strongly against it for a long time. This, I know, was never a custom with your people. Life is given as a great gift and must be cared for and not discarded. There is no rebirth for the sacrificed first-born, and that proves that the custom is not right,' Arg said.

A deep silence prevailed, as they thought about a practice they had often heard of, but never really thought existed.

The howling of wolves from the forests to the south recalled the memory of their winter encounter and sent a chill through them all. Death had come near, but they had won over it, and it had been a valuable experience.

Sar thought of the bear in the Cave of Echoes. Still in his winter sleep, he was not yet a problem, but that would not last much longer. Sar had built a cage in which to trap him, but Fer had decided that the creature should be left alone in the hope that it might leave the island in search of a mate. It could easily swim across to the mainland at the eastern corner where the wolves had crossed the ice. If it were to do this, all would be well, but if it were to return with its mate and produce young, the cattle might be in danger. Then action would have to be taken. But that was for another day.

'In any place I've visited,' Arg concluded, 'burial is as you know it. The body is burnt to release the spirit and then placed in the chamber. The position of the tomb is most important as the sun must cast its lowest rays into it, and life will return at some time, in another body shape perhaps, but return it will.'

The building of the burial-chamber had become a priority.

* * *

Saru and Isht were proud of their wolf-fang pendants which set them together and apart from the other children. And they boasted that these represented a 'wolf killing' pact. Even the parents, who knew nothing of this, began to refer to them as the 'wolf children'.

'Come on!' cried Isht, one afternoon. 'Let's go to the cave!'

Saru was afraid, but he knew that he could not refuse. Isht was beaming in anticipation of adventure. He knew she would go without him if he refused and was fearful of what might happen to her. The fact that he carried a bow and two arrows now gave him a stature that forbade him to show any signs of fear. It was a small bow and the arrows were bone-tipped, intended for practice, certainly not for wild game.

'The bear should be awake by now. He'll be hungry and dangerous,' he said, as they set off across the hill, having made sure that no one saw them leave.

'I only want to see him again,' Isht replied, adding, 'You are going to kill him for me when you're a great hunter?'

A twinge of anger rose in Saru, but their eyes met and it was gone.

They approached the cave cautiously, not seeing any sign of the bear. They edged closer and over the threshold, carried forward on a wave of excitement and fear.

'We should have brought dogs,' Saru whispered. 'It's not safe here. Come on, we've seen enough!'

'But he's not here,' Isht persisted. 'It's safe. We can tell the others that it's time to set Sar's cage – if he hasn't already crossed to the mainland.'

'I don't like it, Isht,' Saru pleaded. 'Come on. Let's go.'

But Isht stepped further into the cave. There was a strong bear smell. Both of them twitched their nostrils in the pungent air. At the back of the cave, even in the dim light, they could see where the bear had slept. The floor was flattened smooth and tufts of fur lay here and there.

'This must be the bear in Yan's story,' Isht said, a little louder, and a slight echo sounded.

Saru was on one knee feeling the ground where the bear had slept. 'There's still heat in it. He hasn't been gone long – and look at the claw marks on the wall!'

Darkness fell. The light from the mouth of the cave blotted out.

'The bear!' Isht screamed. Her cry was answered by a growl that shook the hillside.

'Get behind me!' Saru shouted, pulling Isht back as the growling silhouette approached.

The effort was futile, but Saru hoped it might work. His arrow only drew another, angrier growl. He never had time to release a second shot. The sweeping claws broke his neck, and threw him to one side before reaching Isht.

Their screams and the roars of the bear echoed round the cave and reverberated over water and hill to the village. Every weapon was gathered, and the tribe ran towards the cave.

The bear had dragged the broken bodies outside the cave and was tearing at their flesh. There was no plan. No orders were given. Shocked fury drove them. A barrage of axes struck the bear before he realised what was happening. Fiar's axe struck him in the head. From behind him, Gar struck a mighty blow. The bear fell to the ground and Sar and Uish dealt the final blows. The angry shouts subsided, and cries of anguish replaced them. Yan and Ish knelt beside the bodies of their children. They would have to do with their tears what the fathers had done in killing the killer of their children.

Fer was angry. 'We should have done this long ago. We shouldn't have waited for this to happen.' He spat out the words and Fiar felt that the words were directed at him and he became sad. But it was too late now.

'Skin the beast,' Fer ordered. 'Dig a grave by the shore. Wrap Saru and Isht in the skin. They'll come again as great hunters.'

As the bodies were laid on the skin, their wolf fang pendants stood out. The men's chant of death, led by Sen, rose above the women's wailing as the bodies were buried.

'We need the great tomb now, but it hasn't been built. Someone else will be first to occupy it,' said Fer, and a deep tiredness came over him.

'We must continue with our work, and be free of sadness before the spring celebration,' he confided to Sen as they turned heavy-hearted back to the village.

Chapter 15

The days and nights evened in length, and it was time to celebrate spring with its promise of continuing life. Now the land took on a new appearance as a lush greenness transformed the blanched hills. The tribe exulted in the life about them and looked forward to the day of celebration that would mark Deir's arrival as Gar's companion. They also looked forward to the fertility rite, which would be celebrated late on that night. This year there were no young members to be initiated, but the children were growing fast and there were likely to be one, or even two couples, when this time of year came again.

The weather had been kind, and the planting was speedily done. Preparations for the celebration were begun. The women had acquired dyes from Arg and with these they had coloured some of their clothes. The effect was wonderful. Skin colouring from last year's berries had been stored carefully for just such a celebration, and the women, especially the younger ones, had crushed the wild flowers of last summer to extract the sweet scents which they knew appealed to their men. Such natural cosmetics were important to the women, and even though the men did not generally comment, and certainly not in public, they were pleased when their women dressed themselves well.

Tribal honour was at stake, and so Fer and Sen set out on a final inspection the evening before the visitors were due, which was also the eve of the spring festival. They were pleased with what they saw and praised the tribe. The grain patches beside the houses were orderly, and here and there the first of the seedlings were beginning to appear, a sight which augured well. The big communal patch commanded an impressive position on the hillside facing the midday sun and, as it was the first thing to catch the eye, would impress the visitors. Above the patch, vines transported carefully from the homeland, were taking root, and Cre was confident that they too would flourish and yield a harvest of liquid strength. The midden heaps had been cleared from outside the doors, and the picture was one of snug tidiness and comfort as the houses nestled into their surroundings, the half-year of their standing having mellowed their newness.

The afternoon was glorious as the sun shone down from a clear sky. The world was alive with activity. Here and there on the water's edge the ducks were already hatching, and the swans were hard at work, raising their nests high above the water level. The land-birds were equally busy and, as they flew hither and thither, their song filled the air and left a feeling of happiness.

Beside each house stood a plentiful supply of firewood, and Fer and Sen knew that there was plenty of food ready for cooking on the morrow. The main fire was built up ready for flame. Jars of various sizes, each with its own purpose, sat outside the houses to be heated in the sun and perhaps to display varying prosperities. They also indicated the lack of need among the community. Nobody was ill, neither the old nor young, and this was a great blessing. Fer's one fear was the possibility that Deir and her people might carry some illness with them which did not exist in this, their so far disease-free home.

As Fer and Sen neared the shore, they heard the cries of the children as they tried to escape from their mothers, whose strong and work-worn hands held them firmly in the water and were scrubbing and cleaning their tender skins. But the children's objections were in vain, and each child came from the lake sparkling clean, with matted hair, and shivering, to run on the hill and be dried by the afternoon sun.

Then the women went to the far side of the hill to wash. They knelt or lay in the still, chill water, and their long hair floated out from them as they rubbed it with a white stone and rinsed it so that it would shine the next day. While they bathed, they planned what they would ornament their bodies with, and looked forward to the feel of their newly-washed clothes and the chance of meeting other women in this new land, and seeing how they dressed and adorned themselves. It would be a night of early rest as their rise had to be early also. There would be much to do.

* * *

On the other side of the hill, a boat crossed the lake, hardly breaking the surface of the smooth water. Everyone turned to look, calling to those who hadn't noticed in excited whispers. The visitors were near. Fiar, who had set out to meet the twins and Deir's people that morning, was returning. As the boat touched shore, Fiar leaped to the bank close to Fer and Sen, saluted in greeting and received a nod of acknowledgement.

'They are but a distance of two hours away and will come early on the morrow,' Fiar said. An excited buzz spread through the gathering.

'Good!' Fer replied. 'But why did they not complete their journey today?'

'Their laws do not allow them to meet other tribes, with whom agreements of any sort are being made, except on the day that the business is being conducted and completed. They have a new word for the coming of two people together as Gar and Deir are doing. They call it 'marriage'. Their ceremonies are different from ours and conditions other than ours imposed, but you will hear more of this later. That is all I was told. Gar and Deir cannot meet until the day on which the marriage takes place, spring festival day,' Fiar concluded.

'And that is tomorrow,' Sen added.

By now the sun was low in the sky. Sen walked alone to the western shoulder of the hill to check the arrangement of poles, which marked the sunrises and sunsets and would form the ceremonial enclosure when the sun set on the next day. Satisfied that all was in order, he returned to find Fer waiting for him by the lakeshore. He was glad that they would complete their tour together. They could share their anxieties, for in many ways, meeting a new tribe was an anxious event. But the time was gone for anxiety. They hoped Gar would be happy and that their first acquaintances in this fair land would bring mutual advantage. According to Arg, all would be well. In the falling darkness the two friends rested an arm gently around the other's shoulder and entered the sleeping village.

* * *

Morning came, and the tribe rose early so as to finish their chores as soon as possible. The first task was to light the great fire. Cooking was the responsibility of many of the women, but they were all under the direction of Yan and Ish. Nam would welcome and attend to the visiting women, and they would remain in her house until the ceremony was ready to begin. The hunters had done their job well, having killed a strong buck and two male boars. The carcasses had been prepared and buried in the cool peat some days ago, and the first task for the men was to bring the carcasses to the women. The testicles of the animals had been retained to be fed to Gar as fertility food, and the women laughed as they stuffed them inside each carcass for cooking. The fire stretched for twenty paces and was divided into three sections, one longer than the other two, the surrounding wall of stones being broken to show the divisions.

'Drive the stakes through the carcasses,' Yan ordered, and the men complied.

Two stakes were driven through each boar. The stakes were long and well-seasoned, but even so would have to be replaced many times during cooking. The men drove them through the chest and hind quarters of each carcass. Now the stakes were handles to lift the meat onto the fire, and they rested on the stone wall, keeping the carcass above the flames. Within the fire and under each carcass, a hollowed stone trough gathered some of the melting fats, which the young girls ladled over the cooking flesh. The men stood watching them work until Yan dismissed them.

'But don't go too far away,' she warned. 'We'll need the meat turned many times.'

'And tasted,' said Uish, hopefully.

'We'll do the tasting,' Ish retorted.

'Careful of the special parts,' Fiar taunted, and the men laughed. Yan picked a brand from the fire and pretended to give chase.

All the cattle and many of the sheep were penned in an enclosure, quite a large one, to the west of the village. The purpose was two-fold, not alone did it give the youngsters freedom from herding duties for the day, but it made an impressive display of wealth and status with which to greet the visitors.

The sun was at its high point when they arrived. The

boats crossed and landed together, and five men and six females, three old and three young, disembarked. The younger ones had their heads covered, and no one could tell which was Deir. The older women attended to the younger ones with visible concern and authority.

The men stared curiously, the women more so. The visitors' clothes were not as finely woven as their own. Arg's trade was evident in some of the ornaments they wore. But there were more important differences, the physical differences common to both their men and their women – the visitors were slightly smaller, their heads slightly longer, their foreheads slightly lower and their colouring slightly fairer. Their hair, too, was much lighter and the colour of their eyes was definitely different. Both groups noticed the differences but looked on them favourably. Good to both sides would come from matings.

Gar stood perplexed among the menfolk, not able to recognise Deir. But as he searched for a sign from any one of the three, his eye lingered on one in particular, and instinct told him that his Deir had arrived. A flash of an eye from under her head-covering assured Gar that he was right.

As they stood by the shore, the visitors gazed around them, marvelling at the order of the houses and planted areas and seeing prosperity in the penned cattle and sheep.

Fer broke the silence with words of welcome. Tan, Deir's father, stepped forward: 'We thank you for your kind welcome. We have come to make a marriage between Deir and Gar. We have brought gifts and animals which are still on the other side of the water. You are new to this land but we have been here for many generations. Our people crossed a narrow sea and moved far inland over a period of two generations. We are most pleased that Arg came to you and told of us. We are glad that we can once more strengthen our blood-lines with new tribal joinings.'

'It is a most welcome day for us too,' Fer responded. 'It will bring much happiness to both our tribes. This is Sen, our elder man of wisdom. Go with him, Tan, and speak to him about the ceremony. I trust settlement will come easily.'

Fer beckoned to Nam. 'Take the women to the house and see to their needs, and give Deir special attention.'

'Sar!' he called. 'You'll entertain the visiting men. Listen for the sound of the bones as the signal for the feast.' And the people dispersed in different directions, giving looks of keen interest to one another.

The smoke rose and spread, carrying the aroma of rich cooking meat. The women who tended the fires were flushed from the great heat, but well pleased with their work. Now all was in readiness. The cooked carcasses were taken from the fires, their charred outer layer giving no real indication of the succulent flesh within. Grease still dripped to the ground as the men carried the carcasses, suspended from the long sticks, to the feasting area. All the other dishes were laid out on the ground – fruit, cresses and freshly baked cakes. Large jars of water stood close by.

'Our work is done,' Yan told the men. 'It is time for us to complete our dressing.'

'Begin portioning the meat,' Ish instructed, as she headed away.

Soon after, the bones called and, within minutes, the tribe and visitors had assembled.

The women looked splendid, their gleaming hair drawn tightly back and decorated with bone pins. Some wore bracelets and jewellery of coloured stone, some wore buttons of wood, tinted black and green from the fire and the grass. Charred wood was also used to darken the edges of their eyelids. They came forward proudly, leading their children, their pride touched by the humility of dependence that characterised their position in the tribe.

The feast was a great success, they ate and drank until they could do so no longer. And Fer made a surprising discovery: the visitors had never tasted wine, nor any other fermented drink. Fer and the others looked wistfully at their vine seedlings and felt some pangs of despair. Maybe they would never grow in this land.

Their remaining supply of wine was scarce indeed. What little Cre had spared of what they had brought with them would be gone after tonight. Even Arg's supply was low and, though generous on the night of his arrival, every other drop had to be traded for, and the amount acquired for today's feast had been costly. Arg had told Fer he hadn't bartered wine with Tan's people as it was valueless to them. They were unaware of its powers and benefits. But Arg had also spoken of crushing other fruit in the autumn and gathering some juices for the old folk. But now hospitality dictated that everything must be shared equally and, having drunk deeply himself to guarantee the quality of the dark liquid, Fer passed the skin to Tan. He hesitated for a moment, but the eyes of all the people were on him, so he raised the skin and also drank deeply.

'Tan,' Sen said, 'it is your privilege to drink your fill.'

And Tan lifted the skin again and continued to drink until a sort of dizziness, a pleasant warm feeling, brought a smile to his usually solemn face. Happily he passed the skin on, then sat down sharply, to the applause and cheering of the rest of the gathering. The skin was passed along the line and soon emptied. Those further on now looked anxiously towards Fer. He nodded to Cre to bring out the wine they had traded for with Arg. Again the visitors drank first, but eventually all the men had partaken. Only Tan could be said to be even slightly inebriated.

But the mood was good, afternoon passed into evening, and the time for the ceremony drew nearer and nearer. All eyes turned towards the setting sun. As it hung above the horizon, Fer signalled to his son, Ferac, who raised the assembly-bones and struck them loudly together. As a body, all rose and walked down to the lakeshore. In the stillness the water shone like a sheet of pure gold, the only ripple caused by the ducks still feeding close to shore. Silent homage was paid to the gods of the water who combined with the sun to please the eye and gladden the heart.

The bones were struck again. The procession moved along the shore to Sen's low chant. Softly they responded, their bodies swaying easily to the beat. Now the line swung uphill, zig-zagging to the top, then turning east to climb to the summit where the eagles nested, rendered harmless by their droning chant. Silhouetted against the blazing sun, the procession took on the shape of a monstrous eel which had left the lake and adapted to the land.

Now the line swung south, and then west to face the setting sun once more and encircle the corn patches and the animal enclosures. All the while the chanting rose louder, calling on the spirits of past generations to bring the blessing of fertility to the seeds awaiting the command in the warm earth. The words were few, but the sounds were varied, rising and falling, now soft, now loud, now fast, now slow, changing from whisper to loudest shout. The seeds in the ground heard and could only obey. The timing had to be perfect. The fertility journey had to be completed before the sun set.

Sen watched as the sun touched the horizon and then dipped below it. The procession would end on the western shoulder where his observations were marked. In that place they would bring Gar and Deir together and, as darkness crept over the land, human fertility would be honoured and encouraged.

Chapter 16

Deir knew Gar instantly. He stood among the men in the waiting party, anxious yet inquisitive. And when their eyes met, they fastened to each other as if they could never be loosened again. It was a happy moment for her. She liked the man she saw and, though she worried about her impending mating, she saw in this older man a more acceptable companion than any of the young men of her own tribe whose fathers had approached hers with a view to marriage. Luckily Tan had asked Arg to find her a mate from another tribe to vary the bloodlines, which were becoming constricted within their own tribe. Now she would live away from home, but Tan had been satisfied that she would be well cared for, and a relationship between the two tribes could not be other than beneficial.

Nam knew that she would like Deir from the moment of their meeting, even before a word was spoken between them. The feeling was more than maternal, in Deir she saw herself as she had been some years ago, and in her she could also see her own daughters in a few years hence. She was relieved. She had been concerned about Gar's new woman, because she had a great fondness for her man's brother. Quickly she became aware of the young girl's anxieties and resolved to help and mother her as much as was needed. The child was shy, but she also had a look of determination in her expression. Nam's growing admiration would develop into a bond which would be of great importance in Deir's young life.

When the visiting women entered Fer's house, Nam gave them water to drink and offered them some of the bread she had prepared early that morning. Gradually the barriers were broken down, and the women relaxed and began to talk. The woman who spoke first was clearly in charge. She had a plump warm face under grey stringy hair. Her mouth was sunken and toothless, but her eyes sparkled, and she spoke with a dignity and pride which demanded attention.

'I'm Deir's mother, Eir,' she began, 'and I have brought my sister and Tan's sister as support and companions as we are wise in worldly things and will help Deir if she has any troubles. We will tell her of our own early lives and she'll understand and know the woman's lot.'

Quietly, but forcefully, Deir reponded, 'I understand what marriage brings and am happy to come and found a new family in this island. I know that I'll please Gar and bring children into the world. This is to be my destiny.'

'These other young girls are of our family and are friends of Deir but they are also of marriageable age. They come as companions, but if Gar is not satisfied with Deir for any reason, he can reject her and choose one of them,' Eir explained.

Nam saw the momentary hint of fear on Deir's face, but also saw how quickly it was replaced with a determination that she would not fail, and Nam was pleased.

Though the girls' figures were fairly well hidden in the loose clothing they all wore, Nam noticed that Deir had strong young legs and her hips were swelling to womanhood and the lift of her breasts pressed strongly against her garments.

This girl will bear fine children, she thought to herself.

The conversation moved on to deal with the usual daily activities, and the young women moved to a corner and held their own talk. Nam overheard Gar's name being mentioned often. She knew that Deir was not cowed by the occasion and was overcoming whatever fears she might have.

When the assembly bones sounded, the older women rose and left to join the feast, leaving the young women alone. Shortly afterwards food was brought to the house and Deir ate well.

Sunset was now approaching and it was time to prepare. Deir was already wearing her ceremonial clothes, so her friends paid much attention to her hair, drawing it back over her forehead and tying it with ornamented bone pins which were a gift from her mother. A white flower completed the hair decoration. Bracelets were put on and the sweet scent of crushed flowers was rubbed to any exposed skin. While all this was going on, not a word was spoken. From the moment preparations began, Deir must be silent until she spoke to Gar. The girls paused to view their work, and Deir sat by the door in the slanting rays of the setting sun as a little charcoal was used to accentuate her eyes. Finally, they gave her some flowers to carry as a symbol of her maturity. Beautiful and demure, Deir sat and waited.

Nervousness returned when she heard the procession begin. She felt the pulse of the chanting and wished she could be with them. When they circled the fields and houses, the chant was loud and frenzied. She felt her heart beat faster and her body responding to the lilt of the voices. The chant carried a message of old stirrings for men and women. They passed Fer's house, and now she was ready. She wished for the moment. Her body was making its own decisions. The procession marched to the western shoulder, to the marked area, and sat and watched the sun slipping beneath the horizon. Sen's judgement had been perfect.

When the older women came for Deir, the younger women embraced her. They would not be attending. She put a covering on her head and set forth, her bare feet felt the chill of the dew spreading over the grass. To the north the lake was dark in its shelter of hills, while to the south it still reflected the colours of the sky, changing from gold to pink to fiery red with wisps of cloud like black streaks on the canvas of lake and sky. From the small island the cacophony of the many birds reverberated over the waters.

Deir and the women were greeted with an expectant silence, a silence that spoke louder than the loudest of shouts. The curved line of saplings placed by Sen formed an arc, the sapling marking this sunset at its highest point. Sen stood at this point. The others had formed a circle by extending the arc of the saplings. They parted to allow Deir to enter, and the women took their places beside their men. Ahead Deir could see a male in motionless silhouette against the background of the blazing sky. Now she was afraid once more, wondering what to do next, feeling the silence, conscious of her fast breathing and of her racing heart.

The figure beckoned and extended a hand, and Deir went to him. Then from the circle Gar came forward and stood motionless in front of Sen as if awaiting a signal. Deir kept her eyes steady on his. Sen gave the signal and Gar began to move slowly as if dancing to hidden music. His head, then his arms, his legs and finally all of his body, twisted and turned, moving ever faster. Now he was shouting loudly. The people in the circle began to sway, and then the beat of the bones began. Gar jumped high in the air in a frenzied pitch and landed on his knees in front of Sen and Deir. She sensed that the moment had come. Gently Sen led her forward and placed her hand in Gar's warm hand. Again everything had stopped, and all eyes were upon the two.

Sen raised his arms high in the air and called aloud:

'As earth and sun make life, so shall you. You will raise strong children in whom the spirits of the dead will live again and they in turn will provide lives for you. You have joined hands, now I join you in spirit. Later you will join in body. From now on you belong to each other and you will share what each possesses. Gar, you will take good care of Deir and keep her from harm. Tan, what gifts does Deir bring with her?'

Tan moved a step forward and spoke with pride.

'Deir brings good gifts, but none better than herself. She brings happiness and plenty besides. She brings two cows, three sheep and three goats, five animal skins, some pots and herbs that will cure ills, and the blessings of her tribe.'

There were gasps of approval.

'Well spoken, Tan. Such generosity is appreciated and will bond Gar and Deir as closely together as it will our two tribes.'

Sen walked toward the two in the centre of the circle and placed a hand on the head of each. The chant he intoned now was barely intelligible, but the tribe knew that Gar and Deir were being bound together, and the powers of earth and sky were being invoked. Darkness fell as he chanted and the moon appeared above the hill to add its blessing. The beat of the bones began, and the frenzied dance recommenced. Now Deir was with Gar. They danced and danced. First a weariness came on her and then came a wildness, a madness. The tempo increased. They held each other closely and they danced in wild unison. Strange passion possessed her and she knew what would soon follow, but she was not afraid. Now she knew the reason for her being.

All around voices and sounds rose to a crescendo, and then just as suddenly – silence. It was time. The moon beamed down and still in the fury of passion, Gar laid Deir on the ground in front of the high sapling. Her sign of acceptance was in removing the bone pin and her hair fell free. He felt her tremble and checked his wild desire, and as her young body received him their bond was sealed.

The rite of fertility had begun. Sen called to the gods to make their unions fertile and thus strengthen the tribe. The sounds of human passion drifted across the hill and lake and the sleeping birds stirred.

Gar and Deir did not go to their home until the sun dawned on the new day. Arm-in-arm they moved down the northern slope and sat above the shore watching the moonbeams on the water. Throughout the night their loving had been at times furious, at times gentle, and the rising sun found them asleep in each other's arms. Their new life had begun. Later, Gar would raise a fertility mound at the place where they had spent the night.

Chapter 17

Soon afterwards, Art and the twins departed. The whole community stood on the shore, and their hearts were heavy. Arg had influenced all their lives in some way or another. Perhaps it was the children who would most miss Arg and his stories; for some of the adults an object traded would catch their eye and set off a memory; for others it was a kind word of his that had removed some anxiety. Arg would be remembered, but by none more so than Gar and Deir.

And had he not drawn their attention to the need, the absolute necessity, of building a great burial chamber? This was a tribal status symbol they still lacked. The time was ripe now that the demands of planting were over and the enclosures could easily be maintained by the women and children. When Fer went to speak to Sar about building the tomb, he did so reluctantly. The deaths of Saru and Isht still weighed heavily on Sar's mind. And the cage he had built still stood beside his house.

They sat on the seat-stones outside Sar's house and Sar waited to hear what was troubling Fer.

'The tomb, the burial tomb is on my mind,' Fer began. 'It is time to build. Death has visited and we were not ready. Saru and Isht were only children, and so could be buried in the earth, but death may come again to an adult and we must be ready.'

'Yes,' Sar agreed. 'And death will come again and again. Through death we live again, but the sorrow of death is not any easier as a result.'

'This cage would have saved the young ones. If only we had used it!' Fer sighed, looking towards it.

'Last night, Sen showed me a hunter in the night sky

and told me that Saru and Isht were there. Now I know where they are – following the great hunter.'

Fer wondered how convinced he really was.

'I entrust to you the building of the tomb, great builder. I could command you, but I only ask, and ask that you do it soon. There is a strange feeling upon me, a feeling that death is coming and I will need the great tomb.' Fer's words were disturbing.

'I'll build it,' Sar replied, 'but many will use it before you.' His enthusiasm would grow by the day.

Beside Sar's house there was a patch where no grass could grow as it was being walked on constantly. But Sar found it a good surface to work on, first pouring water on it, then scratching out his designs with a stick. Sar was respected in the tribe and no one would walk on this patch while the work was in progress. Sar sat down to plan the tomb. Little by little, it took shape.

Until Sar was satisfied with the plans, work could not begin. Sometimes Fer and Sen would come and see the work and encourage haste, as the men were idle and waiting to start on the tomb. But Sar would remain unruffled. The first major decision was taken, based on the markings of Sen. The entrance to the tomb would face the points where the sun set, marked by the high sapling, and point towards the rising sun.

At last the construction plans were ready, and on the very next morning the search for a site began. The guidelines were well known to Sar. The tomb must be on the mainland, so life and death would be separated by water. Death was not unwelcome, but neither was it encouraged. However, the spirits of the dead would also protect the living on the island from outside danger. The tomb must be located between a hill and the water, and finally it must be within the beams of sunrises and sunsets and catch the moonlight and the glitter of the stars where the dead rested until their time to live came again.

Sar, Fer, Sen and Gar crossed to the mainland. The search began. Most of them had already formed their own opinion as to the site, but the occasion demanded a search and much discussion before a decision could be taken.

Gar was involved in decision making because he was of the ruling family, being Fer's brother, and would succeed as leader if anything befell Fer before his son was old enough to take control. Were this to happen, the leadership of the tribe would remain in Gar's family for two generations. Aware of this, Gar desired a son and hoped that Deir would produce life before the year's end.

Each man set about finding a suitable place, each wandering away from the other in their search. The terrain was difficult, being thickly forested with hazel and ash. After a time, they all converged on the same place, and this was considered an auspicious sign.

'This is the place. The gods have brought us all here,' Sar said. 'We'll build here.'

'It fulfils all the conditions. It lies between the hill and the water. It's well chosen,' Fer agreed.

Sen and Gar nodded their consent.

The site was indeed perfect. It occupied the only level area between lakeshore and hilltop. Now the plans hatched on the muddy patch found a location. As the site was reasonably clear of growth it was possible to visualise the varying building stages and the completed tomb. They were filled with a certain awe knowing that they would all rest here finally.

Sar viewed the ground with a practised eye, and the great tomb grew in his mind. His previous lack of urgency disappeared instantly, and he knew that this work must begin at once.

Gar's shout was famous, it carried so far and was so loud that it had come to be used as a signal. So the people in the village waited and waited, impatient to hear Gar's voice, which would tell them that the site had been chosen and work would soon commence. When Sar had paced and measured and spoke of his satisfaction, Fer spoke:'Let your strong voice tell the good news to those who wait. The gods have directed well, and our tribe will prosper through its living and dead.'

Inhaling deeply, Gar filled his lungs to the utmost, conscious of the fragrance of the blossoms on the trees and the wild flowers crushed under their feet. He let a mighty roar which was received by the villagers with joy.

Fer looked at Gar with admiration. He was happy for his brother and glad of his support in the matters of rule and decision. He thought of his son Ferac and felt a shiver of fear as an image flashed across his mind. An image of Gar as leader. Ferac was nowhere to be seen. The fear showed on his face.

'Fer, are you all right?' Sar asked.

Fer nodded in reply, but walked away from them.

'What's wrong with him, Sen?' Gar asked quietly. 'He has become different of late. He has suddenly become old.'

Sen had seen signs which he knew were ominous. 'A great change has come on him, much more pronounced since death came to Saru and Isht. He blames himself. He says that a good leader would have had that bear killed. He fears punishment. Not so much fears but expects, and knows it will come as death. He hopes that it will come to him.'

'If it should, then Ferac would take over the leadership,' Gar said.

'He is young, too young. You might well think of being leader yourself.' This remark made Gar uncomfortable.

'It's time to go home,' Fer called.

A warm welcome awaited them.

Chapter 18

Uish understood stone, but this was an unusual task for him. He was being asked to work on stones thousands of times larger than he was used to. But knowledge is knowledge, and whatever the size, the same rules applied. Uish set to work to find stone of a suitable size to comply with Sar's specifications. Uish went to the rockfaces near the site to study their lines and cracks so as to choose the most easily worked. The four large capstones or roofstones of the burial chamber would be the most difficult but there was much to be done before they would be needed.

The site was soon cleared, and Sar and Uish set about laying out the ground plan. Sar carried a stick which was the measure of a man's easy stride. Uish had many timber pegs and a heavy maul. The pegs were of many different lengths. Now that the scrub had been removed, a slight slope was visible, but Sar knew how to counter that.

'We will mark off ten measures from this point,' Sar said, holding up his ten fingers. Uish drove in the first peg. Sar moved carefully eastwards from it, revolving the stick end over end until he was satisfied that the right distance had been covered. Then Uish drove in a second peg – the north line. Next Sar turned south and revolved his stick four times. Another peg was hammered into the ground. He did the same to the west and the fourth peg was planted. The ground area of the tomb was marked off ready for the next stage.

The men stood admiring their work and speculating on the finished tomb. To some extent Sar's work was now over. From now on he would assist and advise Uish.

'It is wider than I thought it would be,' Uish remarked, knowing that the bigger the tomb, the more work it entailed for him.

'That is because of the slope,' Sar answered. 'We will place a smaller wall on the outside which will give further support to the mound and prevent it slipping in years to come. It will stand lower than the side walls, and the stone used need not be as thick. It will also make this tomb different from any others and, though our work will be hidden forever, the tribe will see it during building, and will be proud.'

They continued placing markers, with great difficulty at times, as the rock was very close to the surface. Then a heap of small stones served as a marker. With a mixture of pegs and stone heaps, the ground plan evolved to the satisfaction of Sar and the consternation of Uish who saw his task grow with the outline on the ground. Eventually it would be an enormous tomb and, as if to guarantee perpetuity, it would have to be covered with an equally enormous cairn or mound. Uish knew that when that stage was reached, his work would also be done, as the gathering and heaping of stone and earth would be left to the willing hands of the women and children.

The great chamber was eight lengths long and two wide and was wedge-shaped. Its supporting side walls would carry the four capstones. This would be a formidable structure. The protruding rock and the small amount of soil augured ill for the builders. Since the structure could not have deep foundations, it would have to link together through its side walls, with the capstones binding the whole structure together. This made building much more difficult and very dangerous. The capstones must slope from east to west as the wedged-shaped chamber increased in width.

Uish was glad that the western chamber, at least, was to be small as it was designed more for ceremony than function. It might be described as a holding area, an interim area between death and full death, and life could not begin again until full death had been achieved. Remains, cremated remains, were placed in the western chamber until touched by the setting sun. A port-hole allowed the sun to enter at certain times. The remains must stay there until one full run of seasons had passed or until somebody else died when the remains were placed in the eastern chamber where the rising sun combined with the earth to reincarnate them. When reincarnation would take place no one could tell, not even Sen, but everyone knew that it would be in generations hence.

Work progressed apace. The men on the rockfaces used the traditional ways of working stone, scraping out cracks and faults with antler tips, inserting dried pegs, and then pouring water on them, so they expanded and cracked the stone. Progress was sometimes fast and sometimes very slow. It depended on the internal binding of the rock, which though invisible, seemed to be visible to Uish, whose selections were generally easily workable.

When the old method did not work, the men used an alternative way, but only as a last resort. They built huge fires against the rockfaces, keeping them burning for as long as was needed to bring the rock to a high temperature. Then they poured water onto the rock from the top. Clouds of steam would rise and, with great hissing sounds, the rock would crack. With luck these cracks could be worked on with their pegs and water, and the right size of side-stone or capstone could be worked out.

'I don't like this system,' Uish confessed to Sar. 'There are too many risks involved.'

'Sen has seen death-signs and has fears.'
'We will take great care,' Uish promised.
But will that be enough? Sar wondered to himself.

Uish's experience, the skill of the workers and the quality of the rock combined well. The quiet days became productive days and gradually great slabs of stone began to appear on the ground in front of the rockface. Soon they would lift the stone to the site, the work-force would divide and construction would begin.

* * *

Sen was right. Death was not far away and, when it came, it came in a tragic fashion and took a young victim. Fer's son, Ferac, was a strong youth, on the verge of manhood. He was now doing a man's work at the rockface and was expected to begin his own family group in the next year. The fires had been burning against the rockface for two days. Uish gave the order to pour the water. The usual hissing and crackling began. Suddenly an explosion was heard and a large slab of rock shot from the rockface. It fell on Ferac, crushing him to instant death. Nam and Fer were nearby and their cries were louder than anybody else's. The second death-wail had been sounded.

Quickly the men rushed to the spot and tried frantically to move the huge stone. Finding it impossible because of its great weight, Uish ordered the men to bring long poles to lever it off the body. A large stone was pushed into position and a stout pole resting on it, was placed under the death stone. The men heaved, the stone lifted slightly and, with a crack, the pole shattered. The second pole was stouter and the stone lifted slowly, just enough to allow Ferac's crushed body to be removed.

The women rushed to comfort Nam and his siblings who clung to her.

The tribe assembled around the dead youth. Parents felt the sorrow deeply, knowing that it might well be their own turn to mourn some day. The thought brought a chill to them.

Some claimed that they saw death come to Fer at that moment. Fer's emotions remained hidden. As leader he had to be in control, even in this most testing of moments. Ferac's hands, legs and fortunately, his face had escaped the terrible crushing force. As Fer looked on his son's face, he saw peace but, at the same moment, knew that he himself would never know peace again. Through his mind ran memories of the joys that his son had brought him, the pride and the expectation, all gone forever. Life would not be the same again.

No one moved. They watched and waited, willing Fer all the courage that he needed to bring him through the ordeal. He bent down and gently touched his son's cheek, and the sigh that issued from him would seem to have broken his heart. Nam stood among the women in stunned silence now. Her life had also changed suddenly.

Not until the first drops of rain began to fall, did Fer raise his head and, outwardly calm, address his people. 'My son has been taken from me and from you, whom he would have led one day. The gods have chosen him as a sacrifice to rock and fire and to inhabit this great house of the dead that we are building. Now we know who will be first to lie within. Would that I had been chosen,' he paused, bowed his head and sighed. Gar put his arm around Fer's shoulder.

Fer continued, almost spitting out the most difficult words that he had ever spoken or would have to speak. 'The rock has played its part in taking this young and precious life. The fire awaits and shall have what remains.'

An incredulous buzz spread through the crowd. Would Fer now give his son to the fire? They stared and saw his resolute expression and knew that he would not change his mind. The men realised that a command had been given and they approached the fire. They began to weave a platform from long lengths of fresh saplings to hold the corpse. Soon it was ready and the men carried the body towards it. Ferac had been laid on a deerskin and Uish and Cre gently lowered his corpse and the deerskin together onto the woven platform. Sen raised his hands and called on the gods to prepare a place for their first dead. As the weight of Ferac's body sank into the embers, the flames rose high around him. The wails of the women rose also. They would continue throughout the night.

Chapter 19

Fer had tended the fire all night, and by morning it had done its work. As a pyre it had consumed the body, and now the tribe reassembled as Sen raked out the skeletal remains. Cre had worked late into the night to make a suitable vessel to hold the bones. It was large and well decorated, as befitted the son of the leader.

Sen did not use the usual incantations. These would be reserved until interment in the great tomb took place. Instead he intoned the simpler form which was used for ordinary ground burials. A great sorrow afflicted them all, and Sen hurried as best he could. Eventually he was satisfied that he had gathered as much of the remains as was possible. The bones stood in the vessel, charred and black.

Nam and Fer were given the vessel and the women's wails reached a crescendo, then stopped suddenly. Cut off in mid-air, it was a symbolic end. Mourning would cease now, but there would be no festivities. A procession wound down to the waiting boats. Fer and his family crossed in one, while Sen took Gar and Deir in another. A grave had been dug just outside the door of Fer's home and there the remains were put in a temporary resting place. It had taken Sen and Gar a long time to dissuade Fer from burying the remains within the house. He could not accept death and never would. The burden of leadership grew heavier and heavier. Later he crossed the hill and alone at last, wept bitterly, but the hurt would not go away.

The fire had done its work well as a pyre, but also in heating the rockface to an unprecedented degree, and as it sank back to embers, the men began pouring water on the rock again. This time they avoided passing in front of the rock, the longer journey was safer. Again the steam hissed as if the rock was angry at its treatment and loud cracks were heard and seen, starting at the top and extending down. Large slabs of rock hurtled down from high up, but most broke on the ground below. Some could be used. When Uish saw the results, he knew that no more burning would be needed. Between what had fallen and what was cracked and workable, they now had enough rock. But the price had been high, higher than they knew.

The distance from the rockface to the site was only a hundred paces, so bringing the smaller stones was not difficult. Sar had built a vehicle, a platform of saplings attached to two young ash trees. The rocks were rolled onto the base, and the men used the ash trees as shafts to pull the load over the rough ground, with others pushing. At the same time, construction was going on under Sar's watchful eye.

The lack of soil was a big problem which Uish would have to overcome. But Sar was resourceful and, in much the same way as he would support a roof in a house structure, he devised a framework to support the tomb until the weight of the capstones knitted it all together. Sar was confident that the tomb would stand firm for many generations hence. He was building it to last forever.

Some shaping of rock was needed, and for days the sound of heavy mauls rang about the hills and across the waters. The north and south walls were put in place, resting against the framework for the most part. Work then began on the secondary, mainly decorative, outer walls. These were supported largely by the inner walls and the gap between them was filled with earth and small stones. In some places, where the soil was deep, a hole was dug and the large stone put standing in it, and its base packed tightly with small stones. These self-standers were most important since they would stand up to great pressure when the mound was put in place.

The pace was deliberately slow, now that the materials were gathered. Most of the tribe spent the day on the site. Everyone contributed to the work. The women served food and then worked with their men. Accompanied by their older children, they gathered the earth and stones needed for the mound. But the women were fearful for their children and for their men. Would one victim be enough, or would the gods demand more than one occupant in the house of the dead? The children were shepherded constantly by their mothers and not allowed near their fathers, who worked on the big crushing stones.

The mound grew to the height of the side-stones as women and children toiled side by side. It was now time to bring the capstones to the site. This presented a greater problem. Now the main form of transport was to lie young trees under the stones and roll them along using the trees as rollers. The system was slow but effective. All the women and even the stronger children were needed to push. The four capstones were ready for transportation, but the largest provoked fear. This stone had killed. Subtly at first, but later more directly, Uish transferred the blame from the stone to the will of the gods.

'The gods chose,' he told the anxious workers. 'They chose as only they can. We must obey their command. Now the stone is sacred for ever more. It is a blood stone – a stone of death, but also a stone of life. It will reign over the tomb, protecting the dead within until their lives begin again. Ferac will be the first to live again and glory will be his. This is a chosen stone, though not chosen by us. It will catch the rays and heat of the sun and use this power to recreate. It will stand firm and shelter us within our Mother Earth to bring us life.'

These and other exhortations had the desired effect, and eventually the stone was no longer an object of terror, but venerated as the instrument of sun and earth and ancestral spirits.

Sen had orientated the ground plan. The positioning of the capstone was vital. The opening on the covering mound had to be perfectly correct to allow the rays of the sun to enter at the time of birth and rebirth. Precise calculations and great experience were necessary to calculate this. Error would bring harsh consequences. If the sun proved his calculations wrong, Sen would incur tribal anger and his son, Senac, would very likely not be allowed to succeed him. So he checked and rechecked and was sometimes sure, and sometimes anxious. The height of the side-stones had been chosen to give an upward slant to the capstones, with the largest, the death-stone, taking the slant sunwards. Exactly positioned, it would catch the beams at the right time. Sen made one last check and, satisfied, indicated that the work should proceed.

Uish was pleased. Sen is getting old and slow, he thought to himself. I hope his calculations are right. But he had little real doubt of this. He had watched and admired Sen's skills for many years.

'Tomorrow we'll be finished,' he announced, but of that he certainly had doubts.

* * *

The morning was a morning filled with expectation. Everything was ready. The last task of the previous evening had been to fill the tomb with small stones. Now they covered the timber support frame, so that mound, side-walls and tomb were one – a solid slope up which the capstones were to be pushed and levered, beginning with the death-stone which now lay ready on the lower edge of the slope. Before the last stone was put in place the infill and timber frame would be removed and the weight of the capstones would bind the structure.

As usual, Sen chanted the blessings before the work began. Everybody knew his or her own task well, for the safe positioning of the stone depended on faultless teamwork. The stone lay on the rollers and the pulling thongs were secured around it, passing out over the western chamber, and manned by Cre and Uish and four youths. The other men stood behind the stone with strong stakes for levering and anchoring. The two in the centre levered and, when the stone began to move forward through the combined effort of the ropes, levers and pushing, the anchor stakes were driven into the stonefill and prevented the stone from slipping back.

Sen, alone of the men, had no specific task, but he contributed his waning strength whenever he saw the need most. Every muscle strained to the very last, and beyond, and only total commitment and determination could succeed. Even Fer's injured strength could not be dispensed with. Putting the capstone in place might help the healing process.

There were moments when the task seemed hopeless, when no progress was being made. At such times, Uish began to think of alternatives. Would he have to send to Deir's people for help? He knew that he would be given men, but the tribe would be shamed if help had to be sought from outside. Should he attempt to break the stone in two parts? Even if it could be done successfully, then the stone, which now embodied otherworld connections, would have been violated, and Uish feared the consequences. Everyone's ingenuity was welcomed and all sorts of suggestions were made. Then Sar thought of putting boiled fat on the underside of the stone. It worked. Movement followed, slowly, painfully slowly. This was all the tribe at work, every ounce of collective strength and energy – to the youngest child – was harnessed.

It was almost sunset of the second day, when the great capstone finally slipped into position. Exhausted, the workers collapsed on the ground, aching and bruised, but happy in the knowledge that tribal pride had been vindicated. Between gasps, Sar and Uish praised their work, but there was no need to waste words. The achievement on its own was enough. Only Sen did not rest yet. With an anxious eye, he watched for any subsidence that might alter the position of the stone. If the side-stones failed to bear the weight, then the position would be wrong. He watched and waited and gave a sigh of relief. The bonding process would succeed. Even when the support frame was removed, he was convinced that the structure would be solid enough to house immortality. Sen sat in front of the tomb and rested his face in his hands.

Now it was only a matter of time before the work was completed. The other capstones were smaller and more manageable and slipped relatively easily into place. Before the last one was placed, the infilling and the framework were removed. When the eastern capstone was in position, the main structure was standing free and was self-supporting. Everybody stood and waited.

'Have we been blessed by the spirits of the dead and the power of the mighty sun?' Sen asked, speaking to the tomb.

All eyes watched, fearful that the tomb might collapse in answer to the question. It did not, nor would it ever!

The people rejoiced in their house of the dead. Their settlement was complete. Little by little the great mound was finished, this work being the privilege of the women who knew more than the men of the shape and miracle of rebirth.

The explanation should have come from Nam, but because of Ferac's death the task fell to Yan. She gathered the children about her. The other women were there in support. She began: 'The gods have told us what to do. From this chamber of the dead, life will come again from the actions of man and woman, just as you are here because you were made by your parents. But your parents could not have made you without the consent of the gods.'

The sound of the wind on the water, the rustle of the leaves and bird-song, was lost to the attentive children.

'The female is Mother Earth. Look at the shape of the mound and look at my shape.' She patted her clearly pregnant stomach. 'Within, life is growing. I hope it is Isht returning, but I think it is too soon. Sar placed the seed of life within me.

'The sun enters the chamber of Mother Earth when it is at its lowest point in the winter sky. That time is chosen because the fear of death is overcome by the hope of life. The action of sun and earth is transferred to man and woman, and so the dead are reborn. Isht, Saru and Ferac will be reborn, but we do not know when.'

* * *

As soon as the western chamber was completed, the remains of Fer's son were placed there and with the minimum of ceremony. As leader, it was Fer's prerogative to postpone or cancel the honours. The tomb now had its guard in residence, Ferac. He would not be long alone.

When the ceremony ended, Fer sounded the bones and addressed the assembled tribe. 'Messages come in strange ways,' he began, 'and the gods have sent me a positive message in the death of my son. My time as your leader is over, and since the spirits chose my son as guardian of the great tomb, he cannot succeed me. Tribal law states that Gar is now your leader.'

There were gasps of astonishment. Nobody was more incredulous than Gar. Fer hadn't consulted with or confided in anyone, not even Sen, hence the surprise. But nobody doubted his right to do this. Fer had led them well, and they would respect his decision.

'For a while, I've had it in mind to hand over the leadership. It was also the decision of the gods. I accept it. For what time remains to me, I want peace, and so I want Sar to build a house for me on the small island across the hill. When that's done, there I will remain and wait.'

There was a silence. The tribe expressed its sadness by sitting with bowed heads and rocking gently.

When the house on the island was built, Gar became leader, and Fer left them. Nam did not go to the island with Fer, but remained in the home with the other members of the family. She still prepared Fer's food and sent it to him, but like the others, she was not allowed any contact with him. Not alone was this the law, it was also his wish. His family was to think of him as dead. The tribe would now support him as they might a god. His presence was of a spiritual nature.

Chapter 20

Summer came and it was a plenteous time. The crops promised an excellent harvest. Even the vines seemed to be flourishing. Arg had expressed doubts about their ripening, but the hope was there. Sen reminded Gar of Arg's prediction and both decided that another source of wine should be explored in case his prediction came true.

Midsummer came and was celebrated. Fer did not attend, and as a mark of respect the tribe was solemn and quiet, but as the festivities continued, the present obliterated the past and only the future and happiness remained. The ceremony of the fire was conducted by Gar and Sen on the hilltop. As the flames leapt skywards, high flames on other hills answered and gave them certain comfort that others were nearby.

Deir felt a pang for her family when she saw the fires of what once was home, but she did not allow the thought to last long. She jumped the flames with the others to ensure fertility. She looked at Gar in his leader's garb and was happy and proud. Later she realised that it was at this moment that she knew she was with child. She knew too that it would be a boy.

Gar was an uneasy leader at first and would remain so until Fer's influence was forgotten, or until he died. Even in the peace and solitude of his island retreat, free from the cares of the tribe, Fer's appearance suggested that his life was nearing its end. Gar often found excuses to visit Fer and consult with him, but on some occasions the excuses were so meagre that Fer rebuked him. Sen too became worried lest the tribe might see, in those visits, a weakness in Gar as a leader. So he had to accept Sen's counsel, and gradually began to think and act as a leader. He also began to confide in Deir and ask her advice indirectly. Indirectly, because the women of the tribe were not involved in making decisions other than within the home.

Once a dispute arose between Cre and Fer's wife, Nam, over the ownership of a sheep.

Both owned identical sheep. They were the same age and size, and both had a broken horn, even the break was identical which was most unusual. Since the sheep grazed on open land, when evening came it often happened that the sheep changed homes for the night, but that did not matter. Then one of the sheep disappeared. No trace of it could be found, even though the hill was searched from top to bottom. Nor could they find a body, or any reports of hunters or wolves. The only possibility was that she had somehow gone into a cave system and failed to find her way out again. It was well known that there was a vast cave under the big hill, but no one dared to enter and search, fearing the gods of the underworld.

Sometime after, Gar announced that further search was pointless. The sheep must have died in the caves, or been taken by the gods of the underworld. Now the problem was to whom the remaining sheep belonged. If there had not been some doubt as to the intervention of the gods, there would not have been any problem, but there was a doubt. If Nam and Cre were sure that the gods had taken the sheep, they would have been pleased and each would have disowned the remaining sheep in favour of the other and accepted this honour. But when they began to believe that she had been lost in the cave, both Nam and Cre claimed ownership of the remaining sheep and Gar was called on to decide.

Deir and Gar sat by the fireside of their home one night Deir could see that Gar was troubled and knew that the case of the sheep was the cause of his anxiety. He would have to give a judgement and his people would then judge him on whether or not they thought it wise.

Deir waited until Gar sighed and said: 'Tomorrow I must give judgement. The moon will be full and it is the time. The gods await my ruling also. Should I go and ask Fer for his advice?'

'No, Gar, this time the judgement must be yours. This is the first real test for your leadership. Think hard and decide. You have seen many such decisions made,' Deir assured him. 'All that is important is that your decision is fair and seen to be so by all.'

'I still can't make up my mind,' he replied, and bent down over the fire.

Leadership is a hard task for Gar, she thought and set about helping without seeming to interfere. 'It was something the same once at home,' she began.

Gar looked up and showed interest, glad to listen to anything which might help him.

'Two people claimed to be the owners of a goat. Tan tried everything to decide who was the right owner. He realised that both were genuine in their claim, but the goat could only belong to one. When the matter could not be resolved, he did the only thing which he considered fair. As leader, he confiscated the goat and added it to his own herd. The people admired him for his stern judgement. Quietly over the years, he made amends to both by way of a gift, giving a kid to each in turn.'

Gar could see the sense in this and felt his problem eased. For the first time he knew how to handle the situation. He would not do exactly as Tan had done, but would follow the same lines. Now he knew what his decision would be and knew too that the tribe would admire his judgement.

As the matter had been discussed and the various claims made some days before, Gar would only be giving a judgement. As in all tribal dealings, disagreements were quietly dealt with and the leader's decision was never contested. Both parties were assured of fair play as far as possible, but in this case there must be a loser.

It was the night of the full moon, the night when judgement would be given. As soon as the moon brightened the sky and the earth, the whole tribe assembled. Gar, a successful hunter, had the right to wear antlers with his leader's garb. He had had them attached to his headpiece, and they seemed to add to his height and give a gravity to his appearance. He also chose to carry a staff and his cloak was as colourful as Deir could make it. On these occasions he always wore a necklace of brightly coloured stones which Uish had made for him. Their shape had fertility connotations.

The clashing of the bones announced his arrival. Nam and Cre were in a prominent position. If anybody doubted the fairness of the judgement that was about to be given, nothing was said, but, in some minds, the feeling was that Gar would favour his brother's wife.

He addressed his people: 'I have thought hard on the matter of the ownership of this sheep. It has to belong to one or other of the parties. I know that each of the parties is convinced of their entitlement. But it can only belong to one. I had thought that a solution would be to kill the sheep and divide the flesh. The true owner would then feel harshly treated, while the other ate what they did not own. So I thought further, and sought help from the gods who I had believed took the sheep. But I did not receive any direction from them and so I feel that they are not involved. But I have reached a decision.'

Here he paused and surveyed those about him. He

could see the expectancy in their eyes, and he knew that they hoped for a show of wisdom which would establish his status as leader. This was his first judgement and would be the most important in his life.

He continued. 'Since the ownership of the sheep is in doubt, I have decided that I will take the animal and add it to my own herd.' This was not the ruling that was expected and there was no wisdom in it. Was Gar going to be a selfish leader?

But he had more to say. 'I will take the sheep, but I will give to Nam and Cre a strong lamb each out of my herd, which by next year will replace the loss of a grown sheep. Now I am the one at a loss, but my judgement will be vindicated if the sheep gives birth to two lambs in the spring.'

This judgement was considered just and wise, and the tribe was happy. A cheer arose and Gar was pleased. Deir knew that her husband was now fully accepted as leader. All his life he had shown bravery, and now he had shown wisdom also. She was glad that he had interpreted her story in the way he had, and yet would not feel obliged to her. Deep down he was well aware of his dependence on her, and their bonds grew stronger with every day and their happiness increased.

Chapter 21

Autumn arrived and the crop yield was beyond all expectation, bringing great joy and a feeling of security that could only come from the knowledge of having plenty. Often the tribe had seen the bad harvests at home and were aware of the hunger which could follow during the cold months of winter. At home across the sea, the soil had supported crops for too long and was worn out, and there had seemed to be no fresh ground left to plant in. And this was why they had moved to this new and rich land.

However, they would miss one important treasure of their homeland – the wine, which was so much an integral part of their life, since the vines they had planted had failed. How would they celebrate when the plentiness of the harvest was being honoured? And what of the other festivals? A substitute would have to be found. Perhaps they could trade with another land for wine. If only Arg would return and advise on the matter! In the meantime, other sources must be sought.

Sen's wisdom was called on again. He consulted with the older women and thought deeply. It must be possible to extract the juices from many berries and preserve it in somewhat the same way as wine. But the grape contained so much more juice, that the amount of other berries needed would be huge and time-consuming to collect. Blackberries were the answer perhaps, they were plentiful at the moment and could be collected and crushed and stored.

Once more the vines were visited. The grapes had formed, but it was clear that they could never ripen, no matter how much sunshine they might get before the year's end. As if the gods were taking a hand in matters, the trees which were most productive that year were the elder trees. Their tiny berries were like grapes, but so much smaller, and they hung in heavy bunches so that the branches were bowed down with the abundance of the fruit. Sen examined them carefully. They would be easy to collect, and, if they were given the same curing as grapes, a suitable strength might be retained in them to stimulate and give healing power. The flowers had for a long time been used as a cure for simple illnesses. When steeped in hot water, the tissue heated the body, bringing on a sweat which gave relief.

Preparations had already been made for crushing the grapes, and it was not Sen's nor Gar's intention to let these preparations go to waste. One of the older boats had been converted into a press by removing its crude seats and boring some holes in its hull, through which the crushed juices could seep into the jars placed underneath. The boat had been placed firmly on a rock platform which would support bow and stern. The collected juices would then be heated and stored in jars, tightly covered with the membrane of animal stomachs. These contained a special valve-like opening which allowed the dangerous gases to escape, but prevented air getting in and ruining the wine.

The rumblings from the jars during fermentation were both frightening and dangerous. Many years ago before the special valved cover had been discovered, there had been several accidents when the jars exploded because of the power of the rising gases. All of these factors were taken into account.

After much discussion, Sen decided to collect both elderberries and blackberries. Two different processing methods would be used in the hope of one at least being satisfactory.

'We will crush the elderberries under our feet in the

old boat and deal with them as if they were grapes,' Sen instructed the tribe. 'Now, in storing the juices of blackberries, we are attempting something new. We have never stored them before, but now we must. The older women are the knowledgeable ones now. They have recalled stories of failed attempts during years of poor grape crops. They say blackberries cannot be treated like grapes. But there is a process. We'll boil them with a lot of water, for as long as possible, and then pour the juice into jars, squeezing out the very last drop from the berries. Then the herbs of preservation are added. The herbs I do not know. That is the secret of the women. The jars must then be sealed so that no air can enter, and be placed deep underground. What is left over, we eat.'

'When can the drink be used?' somebody asked.

'It should be ready for the time of rebirth, when we will gather at the great tomb,' Sen replied, having briefly consulted with the women.

'And will the vines grow next year?' another asked.

This time it was Gar who answered. 'We brought the vines from home, mature and strong and ready to produce fruit. They were removed with great care, and their roots were well dressed in the soil in which they had grown. With careful handling and planting, they were placed in our rich soil and surged into growth. Flowers became fruit as the year progressed, but the ripening was lacking. Now we know that this ripening will not take place at all this year. Our new skies carry too much rain and not enough warmth comes through. This is the will of the great god of the sky. We'll let them stay in the ground and if they survive this winter, we'll know when ripening time comes next year whether they will bear fruit.'

Uish was not confident. 'The frost and ice of last winter nearly killed them all,' he said, 'but we must wait and see what this winter will bring.'

'It is important that we find something to replace them,' Gar concluded.

As always new activity brought excitement and the work its own contentment. Each family worked hard, knowing that their share of the produce depended on their doing a fair share of the work. There was no shirking because shared production was a matter of family pride.

Only Nam, being without Fer and Ferac, needed help, and each day younger members of other families joined her and thus her share corresponded well with the others. Nam had earned respect when her man was leader. Now that he had chosen to live alone, their respect for her was strengthened by sympathy. Fer's self-imposed exile on the island was seen as a trial for her as great as her son's death. Custom did not allow the tribe to doubt Fer's entitlement to become a recluse as his life moved towards its end, but a quiet respect was reserved for Nam who bore her many problems with dignity and a strong determination to bring up her remaining children well. Now her every moment would be theirs, as her ties with Fer were completely severed, except when she prepared food for the 'man on the island'.

The men became more and more impatient as the days passed. Even though they knew it was necessary to help in the fruit gathering, they did so with great reluctance. Hunting was more in their line and the hills called. The chase and capture of a prey carried an excitement which could never be found picking berries. Some even thought that a gash from an angry trapped boar was more acceptable than the indignity of scratches and scrapes which was so much part of the blackberry harvest. But Gar kept them to it and assured them that the time for hunting would come again. This precious sustenance for the tribe ensured survival and must take precedence over all else.

The results of their hard work soon became apparent. Enormous heaps of gathered elderberries were crushing well and yielding copious amounts of juice. The old boat was serving its purpose very well too. The juice was poured from the jars into skin-bags. When they were filled and sealed, Cre covered each one with the wet clay he used for making the jars.

A little way from Cre's house, there was a small opening in the rockface which led into a larger opening within. Above it, and separated from it by a thin slab of rock, was a shelflike platform. It was almost a natural oven, and it was here that Cre baked most of his pots. A fire underneath heated up the area above and, though the process was slow, by keeping a blazing fire burning at all times the jars became hard and usable.

Cre spent all his time beside the fire, and the children brought the moistened clay to him. When each skin had been emptied and refilled, he would apply another coat of clay and the procedure would begin again. The coat of clay protected the skin and yet exposed the wine inside to the heat to bring it to the point where it would ferment.

The oven held up to twenty sacks and, after being exposed to the heat for a day, the juices were transferred back to the storage jars where fermentation would take place. When they were being heated, the skins had to be opened every now and then, to release the steam. This filled the area with the sweetest of smells, and encouraged the men to keep gathering. They could dream of nights to come when the sweet-tasting berryjuice would lift them to a state of high happiness.

By the time they were finished, there were twenty jars

of elderwine fermenting. Because of the dangers of fermentation, a small house had been built to hold the jars. When fermentation was completed, the jars would be taken, half to Gar's house and half to Sen's, and sealed and buried within the houses to remain for a half-year, until the spring festival. In the meantime, the blackberry wine would serve the needs of the tribe in sickness and celebration.

Chapter 22

Each year, the gathering of the nuts was left to the women and children and was usually done while the men were hunting. With so little tree cover on the island, it was necessary for them to cross to the mainland to search the forest floor there and gather ahead of the squirrels and the wild boars.

The bounty of the year's harvest was also affecting the wild creatures. They had become fat and lethargic and, in their contentment, were often careless. They used the more frequented pathways and exposed themselves to avoidable dangers, and, though they were beginning to recognise man as an enemy, they were not afraid enough to avoid him completely. So the hunting was successful. The larders were filling fast, especially as it was also the time when the surplus of their domestic animals were killed. Winter held no fears for them. There had been no such plenty in the homeland.

Once the deer were alert, and they were seldom surprised or stalked successfully. They had to be cornered in a natural ravine, or in a man-made enclosure, which was difficult to construct and which the deer instinctively avoided. Digging a pit and covering it with grass often worked and a single alarmed deer could be driven into it, but, when the herd was together, the stag was usually alert to such dangers and would lead his followers from it. Not so with the boar. Hunting him was easy. He didn't have the same speed, though was agile enough among the trees when surrounded and quite prepared to fight to survive. The hunters had long respected and avoided his sharp tusks, especially those of an old boar. His age was a protection for him, with his lethal tusks and his tough meat, and it was usually the younger boars and sows that were hunted – unless the hunters wanted the thrill of chase and the danger of a struggle, then it was the strongest and greatest tusked boar that was sought out. The prize of those mighty tusks went to the hunter who killed and they gave him stature among his peers. Like antlers, he could wear them during celebrations.

Autumn was now drawing to a close, with more golden and brown leaves carpeting the forest floor than remaining on the trees. Yet there were enough to show a woodscape of gold when the sun shone in the clear sky and the first touches of frost came. But the remaining leaves would not last long. The sun, the tribe knew, was growing lazy now and would show less and less of himself in the days ahead. Nor would he climb as high, as he crossed the sky. The shortening days brought cold and gloom and the fear once more that the sun might disappear altogether. However, this was the fear of the younger folk, as the elders had now witnessed the sun's return from his low point so often that they were confident.

Sen studied the heavens continually. He was anxious because the positions of sun and moon suggested that they might meet. As he continued to track their movements, he became convinced that they would converge, and the moon would cover the face of the sun. Sen could recall this happening when he was a child, and it had caused great fear. He watched and waited and became more and more certain, but said nothing. If he told the tribe, he reasoned to himself, he would be laughed at. Should it happen, then let them be afraid for a time. They must fear the great powers. His explanations would only remove the fear.

* * *

It happened. The day was bright and golden, and the women and children were gathering nuts, while the men hunted. No trace of the moon could be seen because of the brilliance of the sun. But the moon was there and she followed her path across the sky. As Sen had guessed, she would move between the sun and earth. The crescent of darkness on the sun's face, at first attracted only a cursory glance from the few, but, as they glanced again, they noticed that the dark patch was increasing in size. Now the brightness was leaving the day.

The tribe stood transfixed, they did not know what was happening and feared the worst. Anxiety gave way to panic. The gathering of nuts ceased, and the frightened children clung to their mothers and could not be reassured. The men stopped their hunting and began to rush back to their women and boats. From far off, they could hear their shouts of fear. Darker and darker the world grew, and with it fear increased. They threw themselves into the boats, and everything was forgotten except the desire to get to their own homes. They felt they might have some hope inside their homes. They would be with their families, and they would not see what was happening. It was clear that the great sun was quenching and if he did not light again, they expected ill consequences.

Gar was gasping for breath when he reached Sen, who was sitting on a rock among his markers and gazing intently at what was happening. Deir was with Nam, so that she would not be alone. But Gar knew that he had to consult with Sen. He felt Sen's complete absence of fear and this brought him immediate relief.

'What's happening, Sen?' he asked quietly.

It was some time before Sen spoke, as if he was preparing his reply very carefully. 'A great meeting is taking place in the heavens. The sun and moon have met and are holding each other in embrace. There is no need to be afraid. Soon they will leave each other again. Already they are beginning to continue on their separate paths.'

'But why is this?' Gar persisted.

'First, you must know that it is the moon that covers the face of the sun. Rarely is she to be seen by day, since her task is to brighten the night, but sometimes we can see her pale outline. I saw her earlier this morning, but the sun's brilliance blotted her out completely. Perhaps she is angry and taking revenge. But I don't think so. I think that only good will come from this meeting.'

'Will I go and tell them all that there is no need to fear?' asked Gar.

'No, do not! Let them see and respect the powers that control their lives. Let them know fear, thinking that light has been lost to darkness and evil. Let them see this darkness as a display of awful power. Then, when light returns, let them feel that mercy has been shown. Let them be grateful, yet in awe of the powers of the sky.'

The light will return. We will not be lost to darkness, thought Gar, but he said, 'I will tell them that the time of light has returned.'

Gar set out for the village. From some houses he could hear sounds of weeping and lamentation. When he had left, the dogs had been cowering in fear and trying to get into the houses for shelter and human protection. Now they were barking at the new light, instinct telling them that the danger was past. Nor were all the people indoors. Most of the men were outside watching the heavens with fascination.

They were surprised to see how relaxed Gar seemed to be. They had heard some frightening stories before of darkness coming by day, but this was the first time that they had witnessed such a strange happening. The moments of darkness had seemed everlasting and, not knowing the reason for what was happening, they feared, as Sen had said, that the anger of the gods had been aroused, and in punishment the great light of the sky was being taken from them.

As the sun began to reappear they felt the relief of reprieve, and they shouted at the shadow to leave the sun's face and it obeyed. Their shouts brought the women and children out and now, brave again, they all hurled abuse at the departing shadow. The sun was almost clear, and, feeling that it was in answer to their urging, they shouted louder still and stamped on the ground and struck their breasts and screamed. The heavens could not refuse such pleading and exhortations and the sun shone brightly once more. For the rest of the day their joy was unbridled, but when the sun set, there were grave doubts in many minds as to whether he would reappear in the morning. The dark shadow might cover him again. The moon didn't visit that night either and this also caused concern. Only Sen and Gar knew that she had visited by day.

Later it would be remembered as the day-after-the-darkness, the day on which the visitors came. Some felt that they should not have been welcomed, that the darkness was an omen of ill, but Gar decided that these poor frightened people would be made welcome and the consequences would have to be borne.

Chapter 23

The day after the darkness dawned and, as the people came from their houses, each looked anxiously at the sun before a smile of relief lit each face. The night had been cold and a layer of frost on grass and branch shone in the morning sun. The blue sky reflected on the waters and, as Fiar looked around, the animals were hungrily beginning their day's grazing. They dragged at the grass with an urgency. The fires were being roused and the smoke rose straight up into a cloudless sky.

Fiar thought back to yesterday and the fear and panic which the seemingly impending destruction brought on men and women alike. Though his was a position which presumed courage, and he had it, yesterday he had been afraid also. He knew that he had shown fear when he had not recovered his axe. He had cast it at a large boar, not noticing the oncoming darkness in the heat of the chase, when he had heard the screams of the women and children. Hearing his own woman's cry above the others, he responded immediately, and, calling to the other hunters, had set off towards the women and the shore.

Now he was most annoyed about the axe; the best he had ever had, perfect in shape and balance. He remembered how annoyed he had been with Uish, who kept taking the axe back to improve it, even when he had declared its perfection. But he had to admit that when Uish finally returned it to him, it was the finest axe he had ever seen. The whole tribe was envious of him, and proud that such an axe belonged to the tribe. Uish had modelled it, with masterly craft and skill, on the black ceremonial axe brought by Arg.

Fiar did not as yet know that he would never again find his axe. The women's cries had distracted him, and the axe had glanced off a tree, missing the boar and proving itself fallible for the first and only time. It had landed with a splash in a small pond. Part of a deep stream which ran through the forest, it had been formed by the many animals who came to drink there and their feet had trampled the bank. Much of the clay from the bank had fallen into the stream and formed a thick layer of mud on the bottom. There the axe had landed and sunk into the mud. Had Fiar searched for it immediately, he would have found it, but at sunset a stag had come to drink, and, stepping on the handle, had broken it cleanly, so that the broken part floated downstream and the axe-head and haftings had been pushed deep into the mud. There they were destined to remain for a long time.

After breakfast, Fiar called to all the people who were crossing to the mainland to assemble on the shore. He was not the only one who was concerned at having left something behind. They had had to leave their kill, a fine boar, behind, and nearly all the women had dropped their collecting jars in the terror of yesterday. The boats skimmed across the calm waters, the women whispering about yesterday, admitting their fears for themselves and their families. The stoic-faced men were silent.

On the opposite shore, Fiar said, 'We'll meet here when the shadows point to the hilltop.' This gave them until two hours before sunset to gather nuts and hunt and make the day worthwhile.

Instinctively, all returned to where yesterday's activities had ended so abruptly. The men were with the women when they arrived at the place where they had been collecting. Their stony looks disappeared when they saw the work of the boars – jars were broken and nuts scattered everywhere, and many had been eaten.

The men took a sneaking pleasure in seeing the women's work undone and laughed as the women fumed and raged and called all sorts of evil on the boars. But their laughter stopped when the women turned on them, accusing them of not being able to kill the boars. Quietly they withdrew, still smiling at the scene. Their laughter soon changed to anger, however, when they reached the place where they had left their kill and found little more than a skeleton – the wolves had had a good night too. The women would have laughed had they seen their faces.

Fiar used this distraction to walk ahead alone. He hadn't spoken about the axe to anybody. It had become a symbol of his hunting prowess, and there had been rumours that it had magical powers and couldn't miss its target. It had missed yesterday but only Fiar knew this, he had been alone at the time. As soon as he found the axe, the myth could continue. He had divided emotions on the matter. Was the skill his, or did the axe have this power? Sometimes he wasn't sure because he was conscious of its very great accuracy. Lately, he had begun to use it only when he knew he couldn't miss. He was enjoying the aura it brought. He always carried at least three other axes – fallible ones – to keep his feet on the ground, as it were.

He strode quickly through the forest, familiar with the path, knowing exactly where to go. Glancing back, he knew that the others would follow him shortly. But he should have sufficient time, even if he had to search a little. He didn't foresee any difficulty. The many animal tracks caught his trained eye, but he kept going until he reached the place. He thought back. The shouts of fear had distracted him as he flung the axe at the boar. He had had time to notice that it had missed its mark and had felt an instant of surprise. Now he remembered seeing the axe strike a tree just as he turned and ordered the retreat.

Fiar walked to the tree and worked out the path of deflection. The sharp edge had sliced through the bark. He stopped and looked about, expecting to see the axe, but no! The undergrowth was sparse and its fallen leaf cover heavy. He began his search.

Neither Fiar nor any of the others ever judged the deflection of the axe correctly. When they joined him, he told them only that he had lost an axe and showed them where it had struck the tree. He did not tell them which axe he had lost. He had always kept a cover on the head of his special axe, and he put this cover on an axe of a similar size so nobody would suspect as yet. They searched and searched. Eventually they were convinced that Fiar was imagining things, but not even he imagined that the axe could have reached the stream.

Not wanting to make a major issue of his loss, Fiar calmly dismissed the matter and called off the search. Axes were often lost and Uish could replace them. Meeting Uish's glance, Fiar realised that Uish knew which axe had been lost. Could he ever replace it? Later, later! Fiar gave the order to recommence hunting.

Outwardly he was calm, but inside Fiar was seething with anger. He wondered what elements might have removed his axe. There was no reason why the gods should hold him in ill-favour. He was fulfilling his position as chief hunter successfully. Surely then it had to be a man. His mind was in a flurry of suspicion and it spared none of his friends.

Uish and Cre had been with him. It couldn't be Uish. He had made it and could make one for himself. But perhaps the lost axe had been his masterpiece and could not be repeated. Then he might desire it and keep it hidden so that he alone could admire his great work. No!

This could not be. Cre was much more likely to have taken it. Immediately he chided himself for suspecting his friend. But Cre had always admired the axe, and the suspicion kept reappearing. What a prize it would be for one of the younger lads who were now hunting with the men, learning the trade. None could have a more prestigious personal possession. It could also be traded discreetly. Or what about Gar? He had been hunting as well. Perhaps he had encouraged one of the youngsters to bring it to him so that he could use its loss as a reason to replace Fiar as chief hunter. But Gar, as leader, could demand and get anything he wanted, since all things were individually cared for but communally held, and the leader was entitled to take what he pleased.

The turmoil in Fiar's mind continued, and he grew angrier and more suspicious. He went with the hunters but his exhortations were so ill-tempered that for a second day everybody was afraid.

I must make a great kill to appease the gods. I must show them that I am still the great hunter, Fiar thought to himself.

* * *

The day's work was drawing to a close. The shadows said so. The women were satisfied with their store of gathered nuts. Full jars had been taken to the lakeshore and many skin-sacks had been filled. Now they were completing the last fills and waiting for the return of the men. They would be glad to get to their homes, to eat and rest in the knowledge that the year's work was done. There would be no food shortage during the winter ahead. And now the birthing time was approaching and rest was needed. The pregnant women were finding the work difficult.

Nam stayed with Deir and worked with her. She felt it her duty to give Deir the same maternal support that her own mother would have given her. Deir's young body was full with life, and she looked forward to bringing her son into the world. Nam, being knowledgeable in the dangers of childbirth, feared for her young friend and did all she could to help her. She would be with her to assist at the birth.

A feeling of unease spread through the group at the same time. A glance at the sun told them that no darkness was coming. Deir felt that she was being watched. She looked about her carefully, but could see nothing. Nam helped her to raise the skin-sack on her back and it was at that moment that Deir saw them. A man, a woman and two small children. As Deir released the bag, and it fell to the ground, Nam turned quickly and stared.

The newcomers walked towards them until no more than twenty paces separated them. Each step brought them more clearly into view. Without doubt they were of a different people, even than Deir's. They looked very frightened and in need of help. They were well-enough dressed in a simple way, but there was a strange sadness in the fear in their eyes. Now they were closer, they looked not like parents and children, but like siblings, a fifteen-year-old male, the female slightly younger, and the other boy and girl less than ten years old. They raised their hands, seeking acceptance. Nam did likewise, and they edged closer.

Just then, the men returned from their hunting. Fiar didn't hesitate. Thinking that he had found the explanation for his missing axe, he drew another one from his belt, and, raising it, ran straight at the youth, shouting, 'Where is it? Return it or I will strike you.'

The youth stepped back, raising his hands in a futile

gesture of protection. Gar moved quickly, catching Fiar's strong wrist and ordering him to put the axe away. It was then that Gar realised which axe had been lost.

Now everybody stood still and frozen. They knew that they had almost witnessed the unimaginable, the unforgivable. Man did not kill his fellow man. The taking of life was for the gods and man could not interfere in that without incurring terrible wrath and paying dearly.

'We are alone,' the girl said softly to Gar. 'We ask for help.'

'Where are your people?' Gar asked.

'They died of the illness,' she replied.

On hearing this, everybody stepped back and the newcomers' fear transferred itself to the assembled people. They started to move away. Gar was in a quandary. He thought of Deir and his unborn child. He thought of all his people and remembered the ravages wrought by illness in the past. But he also thought of the ancient tribal law that ordered man to help his fellow man.

To his people he said, 'All of you – cross back to the island. There's a shelter on the eastern slope. Put it in order, Sar. These people will stay in it for a full moon's term. If illness does not visit them or me in that time, they'll live among us.'

The words were gently spoken, but they were the words of the leader and so must be obeyed. They were all aware of the consequences of bringing the carriers of illness among them, but they knew that Gar had no real choice in the matter. They would have expected nothing else from him. Gar looked at Deir and saw in her gaze her wholehearted support and much concern. As his people moved towards the shore, Gar was left alone with the newcomers.

Chapter 24

'It seems so long ago. We all lived happily beside the great river. Food was plentiful and our people were strong. The hunters took big fish from the great river and caught animals in the chase. The gods blessed us, and the young more than replaced the old when they were called to the other world.

'We were happy, but something went wrong. Our leaders displeased the gods and we never knew how. Maybe they conducted the sacrifices badly, or killed a fellow man. I don't know, but the evil came upon us and all efforts to remove it failed.'

Although Gar had not questioned her, the girl had begun to speak, to tell the story, to explain. She spoke in a low tone with a haunted hollowness, as if her voice was coming from her entire body, rather than through her mouth, and sadness and loneliness and heartbreak seemed part of every word. Gar said nothing. She looked exhausted and pointed to the ground as if asking permission to sit. He nodded and they all sat on the dry warm leaves.

She picked up a light twig and with eyes fixed on the ground, poked at the leaves and continued, 'We were used to death, it is so much a part of life, but it had been kind to us as long as anybody could remember. The old always passed peacefully away. Many infants died, but that is the will of the gods, and we didn't grieve because they would live again. It was harder not to grieve when the mothers died giving birth because, if the infant died as well, neither would live again.'

A chill of fear touched Gar's spine and flickered over his face as he thought of Deir, but still he did not speak and so she continued. 'At first it started among the infants and young children as a cough which got worse and worse. The normal cures proved useless, new remedies were tried and failed. And the coughs got worse and spread to the older children. The night time was the worst. Terrible coughs came from every house, and they spread to the grown-ups and finally to the old people. All work stopped and people remained in their houses, coughing beside their fires, even our strongest hunters.

'I will never know why, but the four of us escaped the illness completely at the time when everybody else was ill and dying. Day and night we tried to help our own people and everybody else, bringing water here and there, lighting fires, cooking. There was no improvement. And the old folk, though the last to be affected, were the first to die. Their throats became sore and swallowing was difficult. We heated our stored fruit juices which gave a little relief. But their throats grew more painful and breathing more and more difficult. In the end their throats closed and death came with a terrible painful struggle.' The memory brought her tears.

Gar noticed the pallor of her companions and knew the strain and shock would not leave their faces for a long time.

'Death came with great pain, especially to the stronger ones who fought until their poor bodies were wasted away. Death came by day and by night. My parents and brothers and sisters died. We are all of different families and the only survivors. Everyone else died. In the beginning, we tried to burn the bodies as was our custom. We put some into the great tomb, but after a time it became impossible, and in the end the only burial was in their own houses which we set on fire.'

Her voice broke, and her crying rose to a wail, which was echoed by the three youngsters. Their lamentation grew frenzied, and they lay and pounded the ground in anguish. Across on the island, the people heard and wondered. Gar placed his hand gently on the girl's shoulder. Gradually her sobs subsided, and they sat silent as the shadows lengthened and moved past the hilltop. They must leave before darkness came. Gar stood up and set out for the shore, beckoning the others to follow.

As the boat crossed the lake, golden in the setting sun, she continued, 'When all were dead, we too, became ill. So we went together into one of the few houses we hadn't burnt and prepared to die. The sickness was terrible. But the days passed and we didn't die. Finally a day came when we knew that we would not die. We decided that as soon as we were well enough we would leave that hated place. We didn't know where we were going, but we had to get away. We took a good supply of food, and we knew that food was to be found in plenty at this time of year. We hoped that we'd meet other people before winter. We have travelled for over two moons and have regained our strength. We're prepared to work and we feel we're free of the illness now. Will you let us stay with you? We'll stay away from the others for as long as you wish.'

Sar and Uish came to the shore and stood a safe distance from them. They had been doing as Gar had requested.

'It is ready, Gar,' Sar shouted, 'and we have put food there as well.'

Gar nodded and set out along the shore with the four. It was almost dark when they reached the shelter on the eastern shore. The roof was in good condition, but the walls were only posts driven in the ground and would not give much shelter, as they had not yet been filled in with mud. This would be an occupation for the newcomers during their quarantine period. Since the weather was still warm, Gar was satisfied that they would be sheltered enough for the moment.

'Until you're told otherwise you must stay here. You can go down to the water, but not over the hill. Your food needs will be seen to each day,' Gar said as he prepared to leave.

He could see the look of gratitude on all four faces. A haven had been found and they knew that they would be well treated by this man. He set off up the slope back to the village.

'My name is Elg,' the girl shouted after him. Gar turned and waved.

Chapter 25

The month passed and at its end Gar was well and healthy and so were the newcomers. But still their welcome was doubtful. These people were different. They had come from a death-filled community. Ill luck was likely to travel with them. Gar sometimes wondered how he would have managed without Nam. Again she led the way when she offered to take Elg into her home and raise her with her own daughters. It would not be for long, thought Gar, as he looked at her ripening body, she would need to be mated soon. There were no further problems then.

Fiar took the youth whose name was Arl. If his decision was prompted by his haste in the forest, it did not matter. He had assured Arl that he was sorry for his action on that day. The two youngsters went to Cre and Uish respectively, as in their old tribe their parents had had similar skills and they would be useful. Then another period of waiting began.

The sun inched towards its lowest point, accurately marked by Sen and his array of uprights. His judgement in the construction of the great tomb would now be tested. Each day he watched. The small opening in the main chamber would trap the rays of rebirth at sunrise, at sunset they would enter the small chamber, which Ferac's remains were still guarding with regenerative promise. Sen had hoped that somebody would replace Ferac, and each time he visited Fer he knew that his time was not long. Fer had called death to himself and the gods would answer.

Three days before the mid-winter, Gar found him dead. The news was greeted neither with surprise nor with sorrow. Fer had died when he had removed himself from the tribe and its leadership. Even Nam and his children had completed their mourning at that time. His passing would go almost unnoticed except for Gar, who felt sadness and the burden of leadership suddenly increased.

Work continued as usual, when the boat with Gar, Sen and Uish left Fer's island and came into view on rounding the headland. A few looked up for a moment, and some thought of times when Fer's strength sustained the tribe, but these thoughts were not expressed. A stiff breeze from the south drove small foam-flecked waves at the boat and slowed progress, but the shore was reached safely and the body taken to the pyre prepared beside the great tomb.

First, only smoke wafted across the waters on the wind, but soon it carried the acrid smell of burning flesh and with it the reality of a death which had not seemed real. Nam stood sadly for a moment and then ushered her children and a mystified Elg into the house. The darkness within and the smoke from the house-fire would obliterate the unpleasantness.

Fer's brother and oldest friends would stay with him and tend the pyre throughout the night. In the morning the remains would be gathered up and placed in the outer chamber. Sen had moved Ferac's urn into the inner chamber, where the winter sun would reach it and begin the process of reincarnation. Fer would remain on guard in the outer chamber until somebody else took his place.

Darkness came early, with the bustle of bird life returning to the lake to rest. The crows settled on the tall trees and cawed long, before they too settled down. But these sounds were scarcely heard above the crackle of the flames. The men sat upwind of the pyre, close enough to be warm for the night. They ate a meal of cold meat and apples and watched the stars come out.

Out of respect, very little was said during the night, but Sen recalled the deaths of Fer's and Gar's mother, who had died from an illness that caused many deaths during a particularly severe winter.

'I will never forget the coldness of that year,' he said. 'The snow fell thick and froze over. When the thaw came, it was followed by more snow which fell in driving blizzards. And because the wolves were so hungry, we had to place a guard each night and by day children could not leave the villages safely.'

'Fer was a strong lad at that time,' Gar interrupted. 'He was to marry Nam, at the next spring festival.'

Sen continued, 'Anyway the cold was too much for many of the old people and chest illness spread among them and within a short time many had died, including your parents. We had so many deaths that the pyres burnt constantly and kept the wolves at bay. The celebration after burial could rarely be held because somebody else had to be mourned. This went on and on. Our losses were shocking.'

He paused, lost in thought. Uish was next to speak. 'Fer excelled as a hunter during that time of cold and death and because of his strong qualities, he was later chosen to be our leader on this expedition.'

Wrapped tightly in their animal skins, Gar and Uish rested, sometimes sleeping. But Sen sat and watched the stars move across the sky and the wonder of the night amazed him.

The pink fingers of dawn finally touched the sky and the new day awakened. On the calm lake-waters, bird activity began once more. The pinks changed to gold as the sun rose over the hill and its rays touched the great tomb. By now the cremation was complete. Sen separated the bones from the ash and placed them in the urn. Quietly chanting the traditional burial verses, Sen, flanked by Gar and Uish, placed the urn in the small chamber. Then they replaced the small capstone and the part of the tumulus that had been removed, making sure to leave the porthole open. They had brought a skin of elderberry wine with them and this was passed among them. Thus was celebrated the passing of Fer's spirit.

The wine acted quickly on their tired bodies and, by the time it was all consumed, the mood was jolly. With difficulty they got into the boat and crossed to the island. But they landed safely and, as they walked up the hill from the shore, their arms around each other's shoulders, laughing, it was easier for the people to forget where the three had come from, and so Fer faded into anonymity. They returned home to fall into deep sleep.

* * *

Gar's sleep was short. It was not long past midday when Deir awakened him. The birth-pains had started. Quickly he dismissed the ache in his head and queasiness in his stomach and held her close, whispering words of encouragement. Then he set off at speed to get Nam and the other women to come and help.

Gar could not return to his house until the birthing was over. Unsure what to do, he wandered over to Fiar's house. He found him sitting outside, fashioning a bone fishing-spear with great skill. When not hunting, Fiar was constantly trying to improve his hunting tools. The four spears of stout ash with flakes of sharp-edged flint embedded in them, which stood outside his door, would surely reach their quarry when the chase was on. Uish and Fiar worked together on many of these new ideas, and already a replacement for the great axe was being made with great secrecy.

Fiar and Gar had been trusted friends for many years. Each had saved the other's life, and this created a strong bond of honour between them.

'Sit down and rest yourself,' Fiar said, as Gar arrived at his side. 'You had trouble yesterday, may you have none today.'

Gar sat and watched Fiar as he pointed the bone on a sandstone, rubbing firmly and turning and turning it until the point was formed and sharpened to his satisfaction.

'The birthing has begun,' Gar announced as casually as he could.

Fiar was admiring his work. Still observing it, he replied, 'May the gods take care of both, but if they need one, may it not be the mother.'

'Come, let us walk by the shore,' Fiar said and rose, striding off towards the shoreline, followed by Gar.

They stood side-by-side for a moment looking across the water, eyes resting on the smoke still rising from the pyre, both thinking the same thoughts. Though the birth would not be discussed, Gar knew Fiar shared his concern. Childbirth was a regular occurrence, but the outcome was so uncertain that he had to steel himself to accept the consequences. Often the giving of life brought death and sadness and this had become the expectation. Outwardly calm, Gar was deeply troubled and his thoughts never left Deir.

They turned the point and headed east along the northern shore. It was late now and the setting sun was hidden behind the hill and dark shadows spread across the waters. The chill in the evening made them increase their pace.

Soon they reached the place where Gar and Deir had spent their first night together on the hill. Gar let Fiar walk ahead and, standing there alone, begged the gods to spare Deir. He turned sharply as the cry of a woman in labour reached his ears.

'Come on, the darkness is coming upon us,' Fiar called and Gar sprinted forward to join him again, disturbing the animals and birds that scuttled and flew away with sounds of alarm and protest. On, still faster, until they reached the shelter where Elg and the others had spent the month. Even in the near darkness one could see how much they had improved it during their time there.

'She'll be somebody's good woman yet,' Gar said.

'In the spring, Sen's son should take a woman,' Fer replied. Gar nodded.

Home across the hill they went, down into the sheltered valley. They passed the rock from which they had watched the wolves savagely kill Gar's cow, but Gar's thoughts were too taken up with Deir's ordeal to remember.

A woman's cries told their own story as they entered the village. They passed Gar's house without stopping and went straight to Fiar's where food would be ready.

As night advanced, the cries grew louder and a tension spread throughout the village. The older women understood, the young girls felt the chill of what was in store for them. The men and women prayed to try to influence the gods and Sen addressed the stars and moon. Even the children slept uneasily.

Shortly before dawn, Deir, by now almost exhausted, gave birth to a strong healthy boy. Nam lifted him by the heels and slapped his back firmly. Little lungs sucked in their first fill of precious air and the exhalation was joined by a loud cry which made Gar's heart leap with joy and brought peace to all the others who waited.

Later, Nam gave the baby back to his mother and as he searched and began to suckle, both women knew that all was well and smiled at each other.

Gar's step was light when he returned next morning to his home, his woman and his son.

Epilogue

To survive the first years of life was difficult then, but Garac was strong and he came through. Gar and Deir sensed that it would be so from the start and Nam often said that his first cry, which was so like Gar's was like a challenge to life. Over the next twelve years, Deir bore six more children, three were healthy and survived, one was still-born and one was delicate and died after two years. Deir died giving birth to her last child. Gar and Deir had spent fourteen happy years together and Deir was now considered old and Gar very much so. The child lived and this blessing greatly lessened Gar's sorrow, because now Deir would be reborn. He was glad that the child was a girl and he gave her her mother's name. Nam was not around to help. She had died a number of years before.

Of the adults who came to Loch Gur only two were still alive – Gar himself and Fiar. Their friendship sustained them and their shared wisdom directed the tribe, which had greatly increased over the years. Eighteen families now lived on the slopes of Knockadoon, each with its own home. The great tomb was being used regularly. Senac had inherited his father's knowledge and carried on the traditions the tribe had brought from their homeland. The tribe had prospered, the land produced well and the herds increased. The cycle of life and death was repeated over and over again.

Elg was to die under sad circumstances. She didn't marry Senac. Fiarac became her man. Being a hunter like his father, he decided to build his house on the hill from where he could watch animal movements on both sides of the hill, as well as the northern, western and southern shorelines. They had two children and the third was soon to be born. Fiarac was often away leading hunting parties and an absence of a few days was not unusual for him. On this occasion he was away alone. He had travelled to a new settlement to the south where he had some trading to discuss. He set off early in the morning, telling Elg that he would be home long before sunset. Around midday the skies darkened and the wind blew fiercely from the north-west. The snow that began to fall thickly was judged by Senac to be of serious proportions. Gar ordered all the animals to be brought in immediately. In the swirling snow, nobody could see Fiarac's house, but neither was anyone worried. He could take care of himself.

The biting cold drove Elg and the children indoors, having searched in vain for the animals. She hoped that Fiarac would soon be home. There was very little timber in for the fire. Outside the blizzard roared and soon the fire began to die. They wrapped themselves in the warmest skins. Still cold, Elg decided that they should try to find their way down to the village, but the snow was by then banked so high at the doorway that she knew that they could not get through. She gathered her children to her, and they huddled beside the dying embers. She thought she was dreaming when she felt the first birth pains. The baby should not be born until after the next moon. She died, the premature infant died and the two other children froze to death. Fiarac didn't return for five full days. He discovered their bodies. Gar judged that they should remain there, and the house was burnt about them. But many others were alive and life would continue.

Other books from The O'Brien Press

THE HAUGHEY FILE
The Unprecedented Career and Last Years of The Boss
Stephen Collins
'Remarkably up-to-date ... fluent, well-written account of a rollercoaster period ... an outline of Irish history ... quite simply, a must.' *The Irish Times. Paperback*

REVOLUTIONARY WOMAN
Kathleen Clarke
First-hand account of the most exciting period of Irish history. About her unusual life with her husband, Tom Clarke.
Paperback

KERRY WALKS
Written and Illustrated by Kevin Corcoran
The book covers the major scenic areas of Kerry with 20 accessible walks around Kenmare, Dingle, The Iveragh Peninsula and North Kerry. Illustrated with the author's drawings and colour photographs.
Paperback
Also **West Cork Walks** *Paperback*

FOLLOW YOUR DREAM
Daniel O'Donnell
Idolised by millions, Daniel O'Donnell became a legend in his twenties. This is his own story in his own words, taking the reader back to his origins, through his early days on the road and his life as an international superstar.
Paperback

DUBLIN BAY
From Killiney to Howth
Brian Lalor
With magnificent vistas in drawings and text. Takes us right around the bay from Killiney to Howth. *Hardback*

OLD DAYS OLD WAYS
Olive Sharkey
Entertaining and informative illustrated folk history, recounting the old way of life in the home and on the land. Full of charm. *Paperback*

SLIGO
Land of Yeats' Desire
John Cowell
An evocative account of the history, literature, folklore and landscapes, with eight guided tours of the city and county. *Paperback*

A Valley of Kings
THE BOYNE
Henry Boylan
An inspired guide to the myths, magic and literature of this beautiful valley with its mysterious 5000-year-old monuments at Newgrange. Illustrated.
Paperback

TRADITIONAL IRISH RECIPES
George L. Thomson
Handwritten in beautiful calligraphy, a collection of favourite recipes from the Irish tradition.
Paperback

THE BLASKET ISLANDS
Next Parish America
Joan and Ray Stagles
The history, characters, social organisation, nature - all aspects of this most fascinating and historical of islands. Illustrated.
Paperback

SKELLIG
Island Outpost of Europe
Des Lavelle
Probably Europe's strangest monument from the Early Christian era, this island, several miles out to sea, was the home of an early monastic settlement. Illustrated.
Paperback

DUBLIN — One Thousand Years
Stephen Conlin
A short history of Dublin with unique full colour reconstruction drawings.
Paperback and hardback

CELTIC WAY OF LIFE
The social and political life of the Celts of early Ireland. A simple and popular history. Illustrated. *Paperback*

MARY ROBINSON
A President with a Purpose
Fergus Finlay
Fascinating account of the Robinson campaign. The making of a President as it really happened. *Paperback*

LAND OF MY CRADLE DAYS
Recollections from a Country Childhood
Martin Morrissey
A touching and informative account of growing up in County Clare during the war years. Sensitive, detailed, moving story of a bygone era. *Paperback*

SMOKEY HOLLOW
Bob Quinn
A worm's eye view of how the fictitious Toner children managed to survive parents, neighbourhood and country in the dark ages before TV. 'A triumph ... Bob Quinn is a natural storyteller.' *Galway Advertiser.*
Paperback

DUBLIN AS A WORK OF ART
Colm Lincoln
From the author of the popular *STEPS & STEEPLES: Cork at the turn of the Century.* Taking the reader from east to west along the quays, and from north to south from Parnell Square to St Stephen's Green, Colm Lincoln provides a visual narrative of how the city came to be what it is today, with the aid of both archive material and new photographs specially commissioned by the National Library.
Black & white photographs throughout by Alan O'Connor £19.95
Hardback

Children's Books

THE BLUE HORSE
Marita Conlon-McKenna
A new novel from the prizewinning author of *UNDER THE HAWTHORN TREE* and *WILDFLOWER GIRL*, set in present-day Ireland. Katie's whole world is turned upside-down when her family's home is destroyed by fire. *Paperback*

STRONGBOW
The Story of Richard and Aoife
Morgan Llywelyn
From the author of *BRIAN BORU*, which won a Bisto Award, another thrilling true-to-life adventure - the dramatic story of the Norman conquest of Ireland. *Paperback*

OCTOBER MOON
Michael Scott
A chilling, heart-stopping story based on the werewolf legend, set in contemporary and ancient Ireland. *Paperback*

BIKE HUNT
A Story of Thieves and Kidnappers
Hugh Galt
An exciting story, set in Dublin and county Wicklow - winner of the Young People's Books medal in the Irish Book Awards. *Paperback*

THE LUCKY BAG
Classic Irish Children's Stories
Ed. Ellis Dillon, Pat Donlon, Pat Egan and Peter Fallon
illustrated by Martin Gale
A collection of the best in Irish children's literature. *Paperback*

THE LOST ISLAND
Ellis Dillon -
Illustrated by David Rooney
The mystery and danger of the sea in this gripping adventure story. *Paperback*

FAERY NIGHTS/ OICHEANTA SÍ
Micheál Mac Liammóir
A unique treasury of Celtic stories in dual language texts and illustrated by the author. *Paperback*

THE LITTLE BLACK SHEEP
Written and illustrated by
Elizabeth Shaw
A simple, charming book to delight the younger child. *Boards*

THE COOL MAC COOL
Gordon Snell -
Illustrated by Wendy Shea
The life and times of legendary Celtic hero Finn MacCool. *Paperback*

BRENDAN THE NAVIGATOR
Explorer of the Ancient World
George Otto Simms
One of the great adventures of the world. Made famous by Tim Severin. *Paperback.*

TOMMY - THE THEATRE CAT
Maureen Potter
A charming tale of backstage theatre life by this well-known entertainer. *Paperback*

Busy Fingers - Art and Craft Series
1 Spring 2 Summer
3 Autumn/Halloween
4 Christmas/Winter
Seán C. O'Leary
A popular collection of simple and attractive things to make throughout the year. Paperback. Also available as a pack of four books. *Paperbacks*

THE DRUID'S TUNE
Orla Melling
The characters from Celtic myths of ancient Ireland are brought to life when two teenagers become entangled in their world through a series of time-change adventures. *Paperback*

WHIZZ QUIZ
Children's Quiz & Puzzle Book
Sean C. O'Leary
Chockful of quizzes (two thirds of the book), with puzzles, tricks and games to delight children.
Illustrated throughout. Paperback

Off We Go... Series
THE DUBLIN ADVENTURE
Siobhan Parkinson
Illustrated by Cathy Henderson
Great fun, and educational too. What do children expect when they visit Dublin from the country for the first time? Two country children experience the thrills of the big city. *Paperback*

Off We Go... Series
THE COUNTRY ADVENTURE
Siobhan Parkinson
Illustrated by Cathy Henderson
A young city-slicker from Dublin leaves the city for the first time to visit her cousins in the country. *Paperback*

CHILDREN'S TAPES

The Boyne Valley Book and Tape of IRISH LEGENDS
Brenda Maguire -
illustrated by Peter Haigh
Favourite legends told by: Gay Byrne, Cyril Cusack, Maureen Potter, Rosaleen Linehan, John B. Keane, Twink.

TELL ME A STORY, PAT
Pat Ingoldsby
Eight stories, seven poems - over an hour of fantasy, fun and magic.

The above is a short selection from the O'Brien Press list. A full list is available at bookshops throughout Ireland. All our books can be purchased at bookshops countrywide. If you require any information or have difficulty in getting our books, contact us.

THE O'BRIEN PRESS
20 Victoria Road, Rathgar, Dublin 6.
Tel. (01) 979598
Fax. (01) 979274